th

Longing

A burned-out trauma doctor at a crossroads returns home to help out at a small-town family practice, a coffee shop owner with a second chance at living, is she just what the doctor needs?

Doctor Adam Sinclair is at a crossroads, burned-out and searching, after losing a young patient he felt he should have been able to save. He returns home to Sunset Beach searching for a way out of the dark hole he's found himself sinking into. He agrees to help out at his mentor's small-town family practice, a lot different than the fast-paced trauma units he's used to. He's not sure what life holds for him. But when he moves into a rundown beach cottage he plans to renovate and meets the ray of sunshine that is his new neighbor, his life will never be the same...

Rosie Olsen nearly died and has been given a second chance at living and she is doing that full force. Spreading joy and smiles with her coffee shop and homemade muffins and other pastries, she is on a mission to change lives. But when the good-looking doctor moves in next door to her she spots a chance to help change his life.

She's just not counting on how he will change her life. And make her want things she isn't sure she can handle.

Can love find a way…will they risk their hearts?

LONGING FOR FOREVER

Sunset Bay Romance, Book One

DEBRA CLOPTON

Longing for Forever

Copyright © 2019 Debra Clopton Parks

CHAPTER ONE

A *man wasn't supposed to feel like a hollow shell.*
But he did.

Doctor Adam Sinclair was smart enough to know it was time to change his life. Time to step out of the shadows hanging over him, time to acknowledge that he needed more.

He needed a life.

Maybe even a wife…maybe.

He just didn't have the heart for finding one right now.

But it was easier to think it than to accomplish it.

Right now he only needed this, time to breathe in the salty air as he stood on the beach of Sunset Bay, with the heat of a crisp January day warming his skin. The feel of that warmth spreading though him, beginning the difficult task of chasing away the chill that encased his soul these days.

When he'd packed up his belongings and left Chicago two months ago, the wind had cut through him and the snow and ice still seemed to cling to him on the inside. It was good to be home, surrounded by the beauty of the Florida coast, with its warmth and sparkling blue water. Momentarily, he wondered why he'd ever left.

Of course, he knew the answer to that—he'd wanted to be a trauma doctor, and in this sleepy little strip of Florida, there wasn't a lot of trauma going on. His career had taken him to some of the biggest and best hospitals across the country: first L.A., then New York, and his last stop—the one where his whirlwind, burn-the-candle-at-both-ends career had caught up with him—Chicago. His reputation as one of the best trauma doctors in the country had made him highly sought-after and consulted with. It was everything he'd ever dreamed of or wanted.

And he'd recently walked away from it all.

Now, he wasn't sure he could ever set foot in a trauma unit again.

But could he do family practice?

Breathing in the salty air, he turned to face his older brother, Tate. Tate looked a lot like him, with their matching sandy-brown hair and gray-blue eyes, square chins and high cheekbones. He was a little taller than Tate, but Tate was broader in the shoulders and chest than Adam, partly due to his strenuous life in his outdoor pursuits and his weight training to keep in shape for his sometimes role as a stuntman. Their mother used to say both of them were too handsome for their own good, Adam with dimples and Tate with his crooked grin. Adam didn't think much about his face very often, but he knew that he was decent-looking, if the women who often stared at him were any indication. To be truthful, their attention was a little unnerving sometimes. To him. He was fairly certain it didn't faze Tate.

He had never been as outgoing as Tate. He preferred a quieter corner to dwell in while Tate had always been the outgoing one. But his more internalized temperament had always been his strongest, or one of his strongest, assets in the trauma unit. He had the ability to keep a clear head, steady hands, and make decisions to act or to pull back. But in both New York and Chicago—Chicago especially— he'd learned that those assets didn't always mean his patient was going to live. The thoughts soured his stomach. He let his gaze shift back to the blue waters.

"What have you decided? Are you going to help out at the clinic?" Tate knew not to push. But they'd been standing here for a while as Adam had stared out at the water, contemplating what he should do.

This was not a time when Adam's usual good judgment was coming into play, and the answers he sought were not coming to him. There was too much turmoil roiling inside him.

He sighed. Why not? "It's just for a couple of days a week, right?" He could feel his blood pressure rising just thinking about walking into a hospital or clinic.

"Just two days a week. Doc Coleman needs a little time off. He's not getting any younger. I mean, he was our doctor from as far back as I can remember, and he was old then..." He paused. Concern filled his eyes. "Look, I know something happened in Chicago. We all know and we're all worried about you. We're very glad you're home, especially since we weren't sure you were coming home when you decided to go visit the cousins in Windswept Bay first. But I told Mom that if you went there first to hang out with Max, Trent, and Jake, you had a reason. Chicago has been in the news constantly, with far more violence than any city deserves. I figure with you working the trauma unit, you had to have been busy. I know Max, Trent, and Jake each had to readjust to life after leaving the military. I figure you had something in common with them, with some of the things you've told me over the phone through the years that you dealt with in the trauma unit. I'm hoping they were able to help you."

Tate had always been observant and right now he was pretty close to the mark. Too close.

Adam raked his hand through his hair. "Let's just

say Chicago wore me down. I became a doctor to save people. Heal people. And as far as I can figure, that's not what I was doing." He'd seen so much senseless violence. So much.

"I hear you, brother. And don't beat up on yourself for having compassion. Stuff like that would get anybody down. Especially someone whose life is dedicated to healing people. But you and I both know that what you were doing and what you would be doing at Doctor Coleman's clinic are not the same thing. At the clinic, you'll be treating fishhooks in fingers, kids with colds and scraped knees. You're going to see people getting well and you're going to eat at the same restaurants with them, see them at social events and when running errands around town. Getting coffee at the local coffee shops—speaking of which, there is a fantastic one on the corner near your house. I know how much you enjoy good coffee, plus they have the best orange marmalade muffins I've ever tasted. It will be a great stop on your way to see patients at the clinic two days a week."

Adam gave Tate a don't-assume-anything look.

Tate ignored it. "Come on, Adam. You and I both know that you can't be a beach bum. Not with the pace of life you've had all these years, going through medical school and then doing your residency and then moving around so much we lost track of you for a little while there. A slow pace will eat you up."

Adam was afraid that was true. However, he didn't plan on doing nothing. Still, working in a family practice could give him a different perspective on the career he'd chosen. The water rolled in and washed over his bare feet. The coolness woke him up a little to the fact that maybe what Tate said was true. Maybe he needed to see people around town who were well after having seen them sick in the office. While he'd been in Windswept Bay, his cousin Cam and his wife Lana were having their baby. It had been a high-risk pregnancy and he'd been able to calm her fears some, to reassure her that she had good doctors and would be okay. After the baby was born, it had felt good to visit them at the hospital and see their happiness. He had gone to the nursery and held the baby and felt the little life in his hands. Holding that baby had helped him feel something… In the trauma unit, holding babies wasn't usually part of the bargain. Was a slower calling what he needed now? Family practice could potentially be as good for him as this warm sunshine and peaceful seaside. He had hopes he could move forward, to come to terms with what had happened…he couldn't go there right now, though. Couldn't think about that last night before he'd known he was done.

"Two days a week? I'll do it. Doc Coleman inspired me to become a doctor and this can be my way of paying him back for that. But no more than that right now. I've been nearly running twenty hours a day for the last ten years and I need some time. That's doctor's orders."

* * *

"Sunshine, oh my little sunshines," Rosie Olsen said in a singsong voice full of excitement as she pulled a tray of fresh orange marmalade muffins from the oven. Their citrus aroma had already filled the coffee shop, but now its mouthwatering scent pretty much kicked the front door open and anyone within twenty feet of the bakery probably smelled them. Which was always what she was counting on.

She smiled as she set them on the cooling rack. "Never fear, my little sweets. You are going to be well-loved. People will come from far and wide to taste your goodness."

Behind her, Lulu Raintree laughed. "Girl, I may love them but if you keep making sinful delicacies like those, my thighs are not going to love you, or me. I swear, I'm going to have to stop coming by here on my way to work every morning."

"*Blasphemy,*" Rosie gasped to the muffins. "Cover your ears, pretty babies. She speaks lies." Picking one of the large golden-topped muffins up, she turned and tilted it back and forth temptingly at Lulu. "Do you want one? They're as delicious as they smell, I can promise you." Rosie knew this because they were one of her patrons' favorites and her favorite too. "They're made of the freshest ingredients, very healthy and not sinful at all. Besides, as my mama would say, if you really, really love something, then the calories don't count." That was something her mother had always told her when she was growing up, when she was teaching her to bake.

"Unfortunately, that's not true, but I wish it was. It certainly sounds good."

"Sad, but true. But, with as many miles as you walk those dogs every day, this muffin is going to slide right off your hips. Unfortunately, I can't say the same, so I'm not having one."

Lulu bit her lip and took a deep breath as she thought about the muffins. "You do have a point. I *do* walk some miles. Half the time the dogs are dragging me." She chuckled. "Still, ever since you opened up this coffee shop so close to my apartment building, it is just too tempting for me not to stop by and get a coffee and morning muffins. It's become a habit. I'm chanting *resist, resist, resist* all the way over here each morning. Then I say, 'give me my usual Americano and one of those, please.'"

Rosie dramatically set the muffin in front of her friend. "I'll say good choice and thank you for your business. I'll get that Americano for you." She spun and went to her sparkling machine of coffee magic and proceeded to make the coffee in a to-go cup.

"You love this, don't you?" Lulu said, her voice muffled as she talked over the mouthful of muffin.

"I do love my coffee shop because I get to feed people delicious baked goods and breakfast items and lunch items. It makes them happy." She carried the steaming cup of coffee to the counter and set it in front of Lulu, who was in the middle of taking another bite of her muffin. "And I really love selling muffins to customers who think they don't want one, then woof them down in three bites." She laughed at her friend.

"That would be me." Lulu chuckled, laid her ten on the counter and took a sip of coffee as Rosie rang up her bill. "So good," she said with a satisfied sigh. "You are a miracle worker. I think it's your love of this place that is the secret ingredient."

"Oh, I *like* that. I need to figure out how to use that in my marketing."

"Speaking of marketing, are you going to have a lot of muffins at your booth at the festival this weekend? You're going to need a lot."

"I'll have a good many. We're going to start baking nonstop the day before. Gigi is working all day to help out."

"Perfect. It's going to be fun and we're expecting a lot of people, so it will help get your name out more. I want you to succeed big-time, so I don't have to worry you're going to close up shop and leave me hanging."

"Aw, that is so sweet. I'm not going anywhere. The corner of Seashell and Main is stuck with me. I'm spreading the word, with complementary muffins somewhere every day."

"Oh, that's a great idea."

The shop had only been open a little longer than two months but she was doing a decent business. Every muffin, Danish, and cookie needed to be perfect because even though she was on a prime spot on the Sunset Bay seawall and beach strip, word-of-mouth would build her business faster than anything. The festival would be a good day. Her social media presence was growing, but still, word-of-mouth was the best after a person tasted her coffee or treats. In some ways, she was old school. And she was going to enjoy the festival, too. She loved people. She loved celebrating each day by brightening someone's day. Maybe out there on the street, without the walls of the shop around her, she could touch someone who might not normally come into the shop. That would be a perfect day.

"I'm glad you are liking the area. You're an asset to this little seaside town."

"I am loving it. I adore my little bungalow and the whole area. It's been easy to settle in because Sunset Bay is a welcoming place."

"I feel the same way. Sunset Bay is a nice community to fit into."

"Exactly," Rosie said, completely understanding. She set a small bag on the counter with another muffin inside. "It's a place to fit in, to find yourself." It was so true for herself. So very true. "That one is on the house—for a snack later."

Lulu's eyes widened. "I love you." She gathered her coffee and muffin. "Thank you and despite the fact that I could stay and eat you out of business, it's time to take my first doggies of the day and get my walking on so I can continue to fit into my jeans." She spun and headed toward the door, waving the paper bag above her head. "I will love every minute that I eat this. Especially now that I've sworn off men for good, these muffins are my go-to substitution. Talk to you later."

"Bye," Rosie called as the door closed behind Lulu. Wondering why exactly her friend had sworn off men, she went back to work. Satisfaction settled over her. She had arrived here, searching for a place to belong and to become a part of a community where she could contribute and be helpful. It was essential to her. She had faced death and won...and it had changed her. Now, she had a mission and here in Sunset Bay, she was finding her spot and learning to live.

She was making friends, though she still had a lot of people to get to know. She did know some of her customers, some better than others and some just by sight. She was starting to fit in. And she'd just heard that she had a new neighbor; though she hadn't met him yet, she'd heard he was the brother to the fire chief. She'd met him briefly when she'd dropped a dozen muffins off at the firehouse. She was glad someone had bought the little cottage—it needed a lot of love.

She went back to taking the muffins from the tray and setting them on a pretty dish. "Okay, my pretties, your mission today: you will help me make someone smile today."

She lifted the plate and set it inside the glass counter with the assortment of breakfast muffins and other goodies already waiting for her customers. They would begin to arrive by seven. Thankfully, they weren't all as early as Lulu because she still had a lot to do to get ready for the day.

The buzzer sounded and she headed to the oven to pull out a fresh batch of muffins. She pulled the large pan from the oven and set it in the cooling rack as the warm scents of cranberry and vanilla wafted through the air. She inhaled deeply, smiling…it was going to be a good day. She could feel it. Then again, every day was a good day, but she just had a feeling that today something special was coming. And when she got that feeling, it was usually right.

CHAPTER TWO

It was a beautiful eighty-degree day with the sun beaming down on Adam, the sound of the waves mixed with the call of the seagulls overhead. Perfect for wade fishing. Adam set his five-gallon bucket full of water and bait fish on the sand outside his bungalow. He carried the decent-sized redfish he'd caught earlier inside the house and placed it in the kitchen sink. He was looking forward to having fresh seafood tonight. He'd spent the afternoon fishing on the beach, walking out into the waves and casting his line as far out into the ocean as he could get it, then wading back to shore and waiting for something to bite. It had been a relaxing few hours on another beautiful day. He'd released most of the fish back to the sea, only keeping the legal-sized redfish for dinner and bucket of bait fish he would use for fishing in the morning.

It was almost six o'clock in the afternoon and he had work to do. He picked up his power drill to use on the screws holding the shutters on the old bungalow and walked back outside. He planned to start scraping the shutters' old paint off before he fixed his dinner.

He pushed open the screen door and walked out onto the small porch just in time to see that a large brown pelican had his large bill plunged into the bucket.

Adam dropped the drill to the chair on his porch and dashed down the steps just as the bird flipped a fish from the five-gallon bucket into the air, then caught it in his bill. He gulped it down in one swallow.

"Hey," Adam yelled and began flapping his arms wildly, feeling ridiculous as he moved toward the pelican.

Not scared at all, the pelican spread its wide wings and flapped them forcefully at him as it looked up and defiantly thrust its big bill toward Adam. It squawked and lunged.

Adam stepped back, startled by the aggression. He knew that a goose would attack, but he hadn't encountered a pelican like this before. He backed away from the bucket of fish, trying to figure out what he should do now.

The bold bird stuffed his bill back in his bait bucket.

"Hold on, bird," Adam snapped. "I fished those fish out of the ocean, so you go back out there and get your own dinner." He was looking forward to fishing again tomorrow using those bait fish. He still had enough in the bucket, but not for long if he didn't get rid of the nuisance bird. Determined to keep his fish, he lunged forward, trying to scare the bird away. "Not so fast, bird. You're not getting those without a fight." He flapped his arms wide and hard, startling the pelican this time. It yanked its bill from the bucket and stepped back, flapping its wings—they had to span six feet—as it lunged forward again. Adam stood his ground, flapping his arms and yelling. It felt as if he and the bird were doing some kind of ritual dance as the bird stretched and lifted its wings high, exposing its armpits. *Did birds have armpits?*

Wingpits. Adam adjusted his thoughts. "I'm not scared of you," he muttered, not at all sure he wasn't going to lose his bait to the big bird.

A very feminine chuckle sounded behind him and he spun.

A woman, straddling a bright-yellow bike that looked as if it had been salvaged from his grandparents' youth. She had buttery blonde hair and a sweetly feminine face. She was definitely feminine. Most definitely pretty.

Like a bright light holding his attention, he lost all thought in that moment as he took her in. The vintage bike had a wire basket on the back that held a bag of groceries, and a white wicker basket on the handlebars with a small pink sack nestled in it. But it wasn't the bike or rack or basket or pink sack that had struck him dumb; it was the woman. She looked as fresh and lovely as a daisy, standing there in her ankle-length yellow jeans, loose blue top, and her long, cascading blonde hair hanging around her shoulders. A blue and white polka dot scarf banded around her hair, holding

19

it back from her face, giving him a full view of dainty features, sparkling sky-blue eyes that were enhanced by her top and scarf, and contrasting bright pink lips. Lips that were wide with a beautiful smile.

Wow. She stood between his rundown bungalow and the next bungalow. It was also blue, with white shutters, a bright yellow door and window boxes that overflowed with flowers—he loved flowers in the winter and Florida made that possible. She looked like one of those flowers.

He felt as if he were looking at a painting, because she and the house were so perfect together. It struck him that he and his worn-out bungalow were a sad contrast.

The bird squawked behind him, sending his heart ramming into his throat. He spun back just in time to see the bird dump his bucket over and his fish spill out onto the sand.

"Oh, no you don't, bird," he yelled, moving toward the bird as it reached for another fish. The bird plucked up the bait fish, tossed it into the air, then caught it in its open beak as it spun away from Adam. It trotted away like a lumbering cargo plane on bad wheels, then lifted into the air, gliding low across the sand and then out over the water, then on to open sea. With his bait.

Adam stared after the bird. "Well, at least you left me three, you bag of bad feathers."

The woman giggled, and he turned back to her. She wasn't on the bike anymore. She had put up the kickstand and was now scooping up the last of his fish and putting them in the bucket. She obviously wasn't squeamish about touching fish.

"You're going to need some more water. Is this your dinner?"

"No, it's bait. I kept one nice-sized redfish for supper but planned on using the bait fish to catch some in the morning for the freezer."

She grimaced, looking at the three small fish. "Looks like the freezer isn't going to get to eat much tomorrow." She held the bucket out to him and smiled.

He took it, his hand brushing her small fingers. A buzz of awareness hummed through him as their skin touched. Momentarily, they both held the handle, then her eyes danced. He'd felt so dead inside for the last couple of months that the spark of heat that rushed through him startled him.

"You need water." She smiled. "They'll die."

"Oh, right." He pulled the bucket back to the side, feeling as if his world had tilted.

"Are you my new neighbor? I live there." She waved her hand behind her toward the perfect beach cottage. Her eyes were dancing.

His gut twisted. "Then I am your new neighbor. Although, there could not be any two more different beach houses than yours and mine."

She placed her pink-tipped hands on her hips and tilted her head to the side to study him, then his bungalow. "That's just the way it looks now. I'm sure it'll start looking better now that it has someone to love it. To be honest, when I moved into mine, I really wanted to adopt yours and fix it up. Bring it back to life, you know. But I didn't have time, so I just had to watch it sit there and hope someone would buy it and give it some love. When Birdie told me someone had bought it, I was ecstatic. An empty house is a hollow place. It needs life in it. Now it has you, and I can't wait to see what you do with the place."

There was something about her. He hummed to

life; something inside him seemed to dance with an energy he hadn't felt in a very long time. He held his hand out. "I'm Adam Sinclair, and I'm not sure about my bungalow fixer-upper skills, but I plan to give it a good shot."

"I'm Rosie Olsen." She placed her pretty hand in his. It was soft and warm and fit perfectly in his palm. "Glad to meet you, neighbor-pelican-warrior-extraordinaire."

He laughed, his pulse racing. "Glad to meet you, neighbor, and I have to be honest—in all the years I lived on the beach growing up, I have never had to fight a pelican."

"Well, get used to it. That's Seymour and he comes around here on a regular basis. When I first moved into my bungalow, he stole all kinds of things from me. Of course, he didn't eat my paintbrushes, but he sure did like to take them and hide them. I'd have to go hunting for them and find them buried in the sand. He stole one of my scarves one time. And a beach towel. He's just a little pest. But I've gotten accustomed to him and I hope you don't decide to try to hurt him."

Adam blinked in alarm. "I wouldn't hurt him. Scare him off my fish, yes. But no matter how irritated I am at him, I wouldn't hurt him."

Relief filled her delicate face. "Good. I didn't get the feeling that you were like that."

The late afternoon breeze held a chill, despite the sun, but it was January after all, so that was to be expected. It lifted the edges of her hair and blew it across her face, and he stared at her like he'd never seen a woman before.

She tugged the hair away with her fingertips, then waved her hand at her bike. "I better get my groceries inside. And if you end up needing anything, just let me know."

She turned and walked back to her bike, and Adam watched, frozen in place as she reached into her basket and picked up the little pink sack that had been perched on top. She spun back to him, catching him staring. Smiling, she retraced her steps back to him. He told himself to stop staring as she held the bag out to him. He pulled his gaze from her face and stared at the paper bag.

"This is for you. A welcome-to-the-neighborhood

gift." She smiled and continued holding the bag out as he stared at it, then her. "Take it," she urged sweetly.

He did, dumbfounded as he stared at the pink bag with *Bake My Day* scrawled across the bag in large script. "I can't take your baked goods or whatever is in here." He handed the bag back out to her.

She shook her head, hands back on hips. "Yes, you can. That's my gift to you. I put it in the basket just in case I saw the perfect person to give them to on the way home, and that is you. They were meant for you." She headed back toward her bike, her long blonde hair and hips gently swaying as she walked.

"Okay, then thanks," he called, feeling mystified and intrigued at the same time. *Who was she?*

"My pleasure. Enjoy the muffins. Talk to you later." She kicked the kickstand up and pushed the bike across the sand to her bungalow, where she propped it against the porch post before picking up her grocery bag from the wire basket and heading up the steps. It took a couple of seconds for her to slip her key in the door and then disappear inside with one last little wave and a smile.

Adam just stood there, holding his bucket of three

fish and his bright-pink bag of bakery goods. A delicious scent came from the bag of muffins. *Had she said she had the bag just for someone who needed it? Or to find the perfect person or something like that?* Rosie Olsen was like a walking bright spot; no, she was like a ray of sunshine and he felt warmed all over as he took his fish and muffins inside his drab little house.

The previous owner, Birdie Carmichael, had used the house for a rental but had decided to sell some of her properties, this being one of them. She had said he had a good neighbor and there was a twinkle in her eye when she said that. No wonder. He had a feeling you couldn't talk or think about Rosie Olsen in any other terms than good. He set the fish bucket down and opened the bag. Two large muffins nestled inside and the mouthwatering scent of orange and cinnamon engulfed him.

Definitely a good neighbor was all he could think as he plucked one from the bag and bit into it. The taste of cinnamon and orange filled his mouth and delighted his taste buds. Delicious. Even better than they smelled. A perfect ending to a good day.

His neighbor intrigued him. He'd worked such long hours in the last few years that he had almost no life outside the emergency room walls. If he'd dated anyone, it was someone who also worked in the hospital. He was taking time right now to adjust to life outside the hospital setting and to evaluate his life. He'd let his work consume all of his time and energy. He'd been high energy, on alert all the time. The idea that that guy would stand in hip-deep water and cast a fishing hook out to sea for an hour didn't even seem possible, but he'd done it for three hours. And he'd enjoyed it. It had been just what he needed. He wasn't sure whether he needed to add dating to his life just yet, but his sweet, smiling, muffin-bearing neighbor certainly had him tempted.

And as unstable a thought as that was right now, just a few days ago it wasn't even a speck on the horizon.

Rosie set her groceries on the counter, her heart thundering from the meeting with her new neighbor.

"Oh, my goodness," she gasped, and tried to push

the pause button on the excitement bubbling up inside her. Her heart ran circles in her chest and her skin still tingled from barely brushing the man's hand when she'd handed over the bucket to him. Who knew simply taking one look at her new neighbor would have her feeling weak-kneed and interested? It was a glorious feeling, actually. It had been a long time since she'd felt this sense of attraction. A long time since she'd had the luxury of even dreaming of thinking about dating, falling in love, and building a future with someone.

Adam Sinclair was one good-looking man. And he'd been about as cute as could be, flapping his arms at Seymour. That bird was a pest, but funny, and it had not looked impressed with Adam as the feathered thief had met his match. She was just glad she'd arrived in time to see the two of them flapping away at each other. She laughed as she pulled a bag of salad from her grocery sack and put it in the refrigerator. It had been a long time since she'd contemplated feeling free to explore the possibility of getting to know a man better, and yes, of thinking about looking for Mr. Right. But things were different for her now and she could do it. Couldn't she?

Her heart raced with the possibility.

Her new neighbor might just be the man to start with. Not that she had a lot of time for dating. Her life was plenty busy with the long hours she worked and the extra things she did after work, with her volunteer work at the Sandy Shores Retirement Home and other various places she had begun offering a helping hand since she'd moved here. Her life was full for now. Just what she wanted.

It was at least fun to think about dating at long last…she just wasn't ready yet.

Then again, she better not let herself get carried away daydreaming because she might get to know Adam Sinclair and realize he was a boring deadbeat. Or something like that.

She laughed at the very idea. The day had certainly been a surprise. And she loved surprises. She loved life. The possibilities, the gift of it, the blessing that she realized it was each and every morning she woke to a new day. She was, quite frankly, a sap about it these days. And she didn't take any one of the extra days God had given her for granted.

She heard a whirring noise and crossed to the window to see what it was. Adam was using a cordless drill to remove screws from the weathered and battered shutters on his bungalow. Her heart rate jumped up just looking at the man.

It was nice, this feeling of excitement and rush of anticipation of what might come over the next little while as she got to know him. Okay, she could dream even if she wasn't ready. Maybe even flirt a little. "You're probably rusty at that too," she muttered, unable to look away.

She was about to force herself to turn away, when a pretty blonde came down the side of the house and he opened his arms. Rosie's mouth fell open as the blonde never slowed down, just rushed into his open arms and hugged the man like she wanted to squeeze all the breath right out of him. She couldn't see the woman's face but Adam's said it all.

"Oh." Rosie sighed, deflating like a stuck balloon. She couldn't help but watch as they looked into each other's eyes while the woman chattered excitedly, making him laugh, and even from this distance, she could see his beautiful eyes dancing as he looked down at her. Then they turned and with his arms still draped over her shoulders, they went up the two steps and into his house.

Rosie leaned over the sink to try and get a view of his friend, but her hair was hanging down like a cascading shield, leaving Rosie to wonder who the mystery woman was. Rosie pulled back and stood there staring at the spot where they'd been seconds ago. "Well, that was one short-lived fantasy," she sighed. But, she added to the depressing thought, determined to keep a positive twist on the day. At least she knew now that she was ready to start thinking about dating.

It just somehow didn't have the same excitement attached to it as thinking about her arm-flapping, bird-battling new neighbor.

CHAPTER THREE

"I'm glad you've come aboard," Doctor Coleman said as Adam entered the older man's office on Friday. "I'm sure it's far different than working an emergency room trauma unit, with all kinds of chaos going on around you. But I appreciate it more than you know. And the folks here in Sunset Bay do, too."

They'd had a busy first day, with Adam seeing some of them and then tagging along with Doc Coleman to be introduced as the new physician who was coming in to help the beloved doctor take a little time off.

"It was a lot different, you're right about that. But like I told you when we talked last week, I needed the break. And, to be honest, it's a nice change of pace."

Doc chortled and leaned back in his ancient leather chair. "Digging seashells out of kids' ears and fish hooks out of men's thumbs is a lot different than digging a bullet out of someone. There's a lot less stress involved for you. And, maybe not the same kind of gratitude and accolades as you get for saving a life, but I can assure you that there is satisfaction in it. At least for me. And sometimes you even get to save a life...or help bring a new life into the world—now that'll get your adrenaline pumping."

Adam let his thoughts go unspoken. He didn't always save lives, and when you seemed as if you were working more in a war zone than a civilian zone, there was a wearing down of a man's soul after a while. At least for him. And then...when a senseless bullet hit a kid and he couldn't save the boy...there was the anger. The anger that had been eating him up inside.

"Are you okay?" Doctor Coleman broke into Adam's thoughts.

He focused. "Yes. I'll be in to work on Monday and you'll be off, right?"

Doc Coleman looked about his office. It was stuffed with books and stacks of papers and boards with photos tacked all over them. Many of the photos were fading or curled at the edges with age. Many of them were of babies. Babies he had delivered. Adam knew if he looked close enough, he'd find his photo and those of his sisters and brothers.

"It'll be the first three-day weekend I've had in years. I'm going fishing. A man needs a fishing trip every decade at least. Don't you think?"

"More than that, he deserves it at least that much." Adam chuckled, though it really wasn't funny. "Go and enjoy yourself. And if this temporary three months works out, you can get used to it."

"I'm, for one, hoping it works out. I'll have to look for someone else if not, because I've made my mind up that I'm going to start relaxing some. But, you have always been my first choice to take over for me. I've just been trying to wait you out. Let you get that drive for excitement and adrenaline rush out of your system."

Adam didn't know what to say. Had he gotten it out of his system or was he in crisis mode? A few minutes later, as he headed back to his bungalow, he kept going over the doc's words. *Had he just been in it for the adrenaline rush?*

No, but it had been a big help to him to keep him doing his job when he needed his skills the most. Now it was gone.

Compassion fatigue was something he'd denied for over a year, but then there came the night he couldn't deny it any longer. The night he'd lost the boy. A hard lump formed in his chest thinking about the poor kid. Adam had walked away and taken a leave of absence after losing Mikie.

He'd known it was time—couldn't go on even if he'd wanted to. He'd blamed himself. Still did. Questions about that night haunted him. He hadn't been able to continue after that and he'd walked away. Now, here he was, back home, where his dreams of being a doctor had begun. Here, he was hoping the joy would return and his mind and soul would heal. That somehow he'd find peace. But the sleepless nights still persisted. Sleep evaded him as he relived every aspect of that night fighting to save little Mikie's life. But he hadn't been able to do it.

There were other similar cases where he'd lost his patient, but in Adam's mind he'd given them his all, done absolutely everything he could to save them. He wasn't sure if he had done that where the little boy was concerned.

And that doubt and losing Mikie ate at him constantly.

Spotting the coffee shop, Bake My Day, that Tate had suggested, and the place where his neighbor had bought the muffins he'd devoured, he pressed the brake and pulled into an empty parking spot. He passed it every day, leaving or coming home, but hadn't stopped yet. But today, needing something to help shake the sudden feelings threatening to pull him down, he pulled into an open parking space and got out. He wasn't a huge sweet eater, but the muffins had been more than excellent and he had been tempted with thoughts of them often.

Then again, it could have been that they were connected to his neighbor, whom he'd had on his mind over the last week and it had always been a sunny spot in his thoughts when he let himself think of her. He hadn't seen much of her since that day she'd caught him looking ridiculous with the pelican. Her job, whatever she did, must have her keeping odd hours because most of the time it didn't look as if she were home. He even wondered if she might be a nurse or something since he was used to the medical field having odd hours. Her yellow bike would be there in the evenings but she wasn't outside when he was, and in the mornings, despite the fact that he did his early morning jog at six, her bike was gone. Maybe she slept days and worked nights.

He had decided that if he was going to run into her again, he would have to spend all day outside so he could catch her in that small sliver of time that she returned home, parked her bike, and disappeared inside, never to be seen—at least by him—again.

He walked to the cute building, and as he opened the door he decided that he would buy her some muffins today to return the favor. And if all else failed and he didn't see her today, he would hang the bag from her doorknob so that she would have the muffins to enjoy. *Good plan.* A plan that upped his mood and gave him more purpose for being here than simply filling his own stomach.

The heavenly scent hit him the instant the door opened. Rich coffee and mouthwatering scents of delicious things being fresh baked nearly took him to his knees, it was so rich and strong. The place was fairly empty other than a table with four older ladies who seemed to be busy dipping round balls of what looked like cake or muffins into a container of chocolate and then setting them on a tray. They were chattering, but stopped to stare when he entered.

Halting inside the doorway, he nodded to them and smiled... It was then that he realized one of the ladies was Birdie Carmichael, the older lady he'd bought his bungalow from. "Afternoon, ladies. Ms. Carmichael." It didn't take but an instant for smiles of welcome to splash across their faces in a wave.

"Good afternoon to you, too. And I'm only going

to tell you once more to call me Birdie. I don't cotton to the Ms., Mrs., or Miss. I'm just plain Birdie."

A youthful-looking older woman with big glasses that were rimmed in multi-toned colors like party confetti, smiled. "She's right—Birdie suits her. And I'm Lila Peabody. You can call me Lila. And this here is Mami Desmond and Doreen Posey. I hear you're the new doc in town. We are too to some extent. We were all snowbirds, coming down during the winter, and then we all decided not to go back up north."

"We are so glad to have a new doctor in town. Especially such a handsome one," the lady named Mami said.

Doreen just nodded and went back to work dipping the ball on the stick into the chocolate sauce.

"It's a pleasure to meet you all." He moved across the room to their table, curious about what they were doing and how she knew him as the doctor. "I'm helping out at Doctor Coleman's for a few months. How did you know?"

Lila blinked hard behind her thick glasses. "Birdie told me. Said a tall drink of water had bought one of her dilapidated bungalows and was some fancy doctor come home to give old Doc Coleman some much-needed time off."

A tall drink of water. The description—and her bluntness—took him by surprise. He looked at Birdie. "Looks like you're someone I need to look out for."

The old woman grinned impishly. "I been around a long time and don't see any reason not to say what I mean. And you are a good-looking doctor in his prime. And those dimples...*oh my.* I might be old but I'm not blind. Those brothers of yours are heartbreakers too. And that one that's the fire chief, he's got those same dimples."

The women all laughed and agreed, making him slightly uncomfortable.

"Okay, ladies, don't make our new doctor skittish. Don't mind them—they don't bite."

He swung around at the familiar voice. His neighbor, Rosie Olsen, stood in the doorway of the back room behind the counter. She wore a pink apron with the words *Bake My Day* scrawled across it and she looked adorable. His senses heightened instantly:

his adrenaline spiked, his heart thumped wildly, and a pleasant sense of well-being surrounded him, even with the reaction. "I'm not scared."

That brought more laughter and made Rosie's smile widen, which pleased him all the way to his toes.

She moved from the doorway and came from behind the counter carrying a tray of the balls with sticks sticking out of them. She looked at what the ladies were doing.

"Great job, girls. Those are going to be a hit."

"What are those?" He tried not to stare at her.

"Muffin balls and cake balls on a stick." She took the now chocolate-covered tray in one hand that Lila lifted up to her and then twisted to set the new batch of muffin balls on the table.

When the finished tray tilted, he moved quickly to take it from her, seeing disaster in the making. "Here, let me help."

"Oh, thanks." She released the tray. "I need all the help I can get at this time of the day. I'm normally in bed taking a much-needed nap about now, but there is too much to do before tomorrow." She spun and started back the way she'd come and he followed, catching a grin pass between Lila and Birdie as he turned to follow her.

"What's happening tomorrow? And why are you sleeping in the afternoons?" The idea of her napping at her age had him instantly concerned. Then again, he reminded himself that she was gone in the wee hours of the morning and her bike was parked at her door around five but then he didn't see her in the evenings. "And do you work here? I hadn't realized that when you gave me the muffins the other day." He was rambling. He wasn't normally that way but she fascinated him and he was curious.

She paused at the doorway and gave him that stunning smile that did things to his insides. "I own the shop and tomorrow is the festival I agreed to have a booth in. But Gigi, my part-time help, had to call in sick again. She caught the flu or something and can't seem to kick it to the curb. And Trena was already scheduled to visit her family this weekend and I couldn't ask her to take up the slack. It's her grandmother's birthday, after all. Poor Gigi feels terrible, both physically and just helpless about the whole thing. But she can't help it, poor thing, but no matter. I'm in a real mess. Thankfully the ladies realized I was in desperate need and volunteered to help me." She led the way into the back and opened a large freezer. "Slide them on that shelf, please."

He did as told, passing by her close enough to smell the sweet scent of the bakery on her. She'd been talking nonstop and exposing just how highly distraught she was about her situation. He was taking it all in but was so distracted by her that it hadn't had time to process. They were both standing in the doorway of the freezer as the cold air swept over them, but he wasn't cold. No, he was warm all over. Looking into her endless blue eyes...his brain fogged over, thinking her eyes were like an inviting ocean and he wanted to dive into them.

He had the nearly overwhelming desire to lean forward and kiss her. She stared up at him and he leaned slightly forward but caught himself. His actions were completely out of character for him.

Her gaze dropped to his lips, and for a moment he

thought she might be thinking the exact same thing he was—that him kissing her was a good idea.

"And, to answer your other question, I sleep or take a nap about this time every day because I'm usually up at four, here baking every morning. So, I find that if I take a nap when I get off or soon after I have done my errands for the day, then I have more time in the evening to not feel completely worn out. And I can do my thing before turning in for the rest of the night."

She gazed up at him, looking like a bird ready to fly. There was no way that this attraction he felt humming between them was one-sided. The vibes jolted between them like electrical currents on a short fuse. He propped one hand on the door of the freezer, completely dialed into capturing her fast-talking, tempting lips with his.

"And what exactly is your thing?" he asked, fighting the pull between them—very much wanting to know everything about her, especially how her lips would feel kissing him. She hadn't moved since he'd placed his hand on the freezer door frame beside her head, but was still looking at him as if she were entertaining similar thoughts. Then her words got past his preoccupied thoughts and rocked him to his senses. He pulled his hand back and stepped away from her, out of the cold air that had obviously frozen his brain.

"You ride your bike through the streets of Sunset Bay at *four* in the morning? Alone? Are you *crazy*?" He hadn't meant that to come out like that, but he wasn't exactly feeling in control at the moment.

Her eyes narrowed, and her mouth dropped open. "What?" She closed the freezer door and faced him, clearly alarmed.

He hated putting that expression on her pretty face, but she should be alarmed because no woman needed to be on a bicycle, alone in the dark, that early in the morning. "Do you?"

"Yes, I ride my bike on the streets of Sunset Bay at four and no one bothers me."

"Yet," he snapped, feeling crazy with worry. "Don't you have a car?"

"No. I don't want a car. Everything I need is right here near me. It's only one block to my shop. *One block*."

It wasn't much farther than a block, but this world was not a nice place. Terrible things happened that early in the morning. Dark and terrible things happened in the dark. Terrible things happened in the daylight, too—at least they had in Chicago and in New York.

He raked a hand through his hair as an overwhelming wave of worry for her crashed down upon him. "Look, I don't want to seem bossy, but I worked trauma units and I see what happens in the early mornings in the cover of darkness. I've treated people who've been attacked, who've been shot, stabbed, raped. It's not pretty. You don't need to be out in the dark like that alone." He needed to step back into the freezer to cool off.

Her eyes saddened. "I am sorry that your view on life is so negative and that you've seen so many horrific things that influence that view. But I have another perspective and I focus on the good. And Sunset Bay is a quaint little beach town where people know each other and appreciate each other and look out for each other. They don't murder each other or harm each other."

Stubborn woman. "It just takes one bad seed to move into town and turn your world upside down. I'm just concerned. And obviously someone needs to look out for you."

She visibly pulled back and took a deep breath. "I just met you. So, I think this is a little premature on your part. While I appreciate your concern, I don't want it. Believe me, I've been through a lot in my life and there's not much anymore that scares me. And after my last round of…well, my last ordeal, I decided I wasn't going to be scared ever again. I *enjoy* riding my bike to my shop in the dark at four in the morning. It's quiet and peaceful. I enjoy that still time in the wee hours as I open my doors, turn on the lights, get the coffee brewing and I start baking. I watch the sunrise through my large store windows as I roll dough or make muffins. I feel peace."

She mesmerized him. He remembered a time when he'd been a kid growing up in Sunset Bay and didn't have a care or fear in the world. But he was an adult now and he knew differently. "I get that you love it. But it's still not safe."

Her shoulders lifted and she sighed. "I'm safe. I'll continue filling this place with the scents that make people happy as I bake fresh muffins and pastries for them each day. It makes me happy and I'm going to keep riding my bike because it also makes me happy. But as much as I love making people happy, I'm not going to alter my routine in order to do that." She turned and walked back into the front room of the store.

What had she been through that made her make such a drastic declaration? He wasn't done, not by a long shot, because he wanted her to be safe. But he wanted to know what she'd been talking about when she'd talked about the ordeal she'd been through. Still, no matter what she'd been through, he was going to make her understand his point of view. He was a doctor; most people listened to his point of view— most people asked for his advice. So why was she being so stubborn?

So reckless?

CHAPTER FOUR

Rosie fought emotions that threatened to send her spiraling. Adam had startled her when she walked from the back room earlier to find her incredibly handsome neighbor talking with her friends. Since meeting him that first day, she had discovered that he was the new doctor in town. She'd overheard Birdie telling the other ladies the next morning at their usual coffee and muffin meeting. They had been sitting around the table in the corner, in a deep discussion about the new doctor. Birdie had then told her he had bought the cottage next door to her. Everyone was thrilled that he had started working a couple of days a week to relieve old Doc Coleman. It had piqued her interest. Her bird-battling neighbor was not only good-looking, but a doctor too. It was, to her, an irresistible combination. She had a very high regard for doctors and a very good reason for that regard. And then add on the fact that he was helping out Doc Colman...the man was a hero on all counts.

Everyone loved Doc Coleman. The man was so dedicated to keeping the community well, even to his own detriment. So in their eyes, Adam Sinclair, in coming to ease his workload, had practically put on a red cape and joined the realm of superhero. He was giving Doc the time off everyone knew he needed, and add to that that he was a hometown boy...this automatically elevated Adam to superhero status.

And he was living right next door to her.

She had been busy since that first meeting as she was baking extra every evening in preparation of having enough baked goods for the shop and the festival booth. She had seen him, though, a few times when she woke from her evening nap and looked out her kitchen window. He'd been working on the bungalow, sometimes without his shirt on, and she knew that beneath that shirt, the doctor was built. Not that she needed to be thinking about that right now; she needed to stay on track. She had been working on flyers and social media for the festival so she'd forced herself to stay inside, not avoiding him exactly, but she had to admit that she was relieved to have something to keep her busy and out of trouble. Because she had been afraid that if she went outside and talked to him again that she might not be able to hide her attraction to him.

Something about the man called to her, made her want to feel things she hadn't felt in a very long time and, well, quite frankly, it all scared her.

Was she ready to try to let someone past the barriers around her heart?

Could she handle the emotions a romance could set in motion?

Ready or not, the man had followed her into the back room and almost kissed her, standing right there in the doorway of the walk-in freezer. Even the frigid air couldn't cool the heat waves between them. *And she had almost let him kiss her.*

She didn't kiss men she barely knew.

And yet she had wanted to kiss Adam.

Very much.

Until he'd opened his mouth and said those ridiculous things. What had he been thinking? He was far too bossy for her taste. It was a good thing she'd learned that now. Then again, she'd also learned that he had a very sad and jaded opinion of the world. And that made her ache to change his mind.

He walked from the back of the bakery and instantly the room shrank around them. She checked the muffins baking in the oven, letting the heat wash over her in hopes that anyone looking at her would think the oven had turned her cheeks red. She willed him to walk around the counter and back into the front of the bakery. He needed to leave. Or at least put the counter between them.

But no, he didn't do that. Instead, he walked over to her.

He spoke softly, for her ears only. "I'm sorry. I

was out of line back there. You're right—we barely know each other. So what right do I have to try to foist my wishes on you? None. But, I'm a doctor and giving advice comes naturally." He shrugged. "It's a hard habit to break. And while I can't say I'm happy you disagree with my cautions to you, I can say I'm sorry that I was so blunt and demanding and out of line completely. Can you forgive me and let us start over?"

Shocked, she studied his face. His expression held sincere regret. She could imagine that his job did make it hard to keep his opinions to himself. She didn't like holding grudges. It was poison to the soul and entirely not good for anyone. "I accept and yes, we can start over. Did you come into the bakery for a cup of coffee and a muffin?"

Rosie, what are you doing?

He looked relieved at her easy acceptance and smiled, then glanced around the shop, his gaze touching the four ladies at the table. She followed his gaze and saw Birdie and the gang watching them. Realizing they'd been caught snooping, they immediately went back to dipping muffins into chocolate as if their lives depended on it.

"I am off work and I don't have any plans. I *could* work for muffins and coffee."

"Oh," she gasped. *He wanted to help.*

She should send him away. She did not need to work beside him. No, not at all. She was too attracted to him. And she had a deep fear that while he had apologized for his earlier words, if she let them get to know each other better, then his opinion would reemerge. Only stronger.

She was a warrior, she reminded herself. She was very strong-willed and no one else's opinion usually mattered to her much, at least not anymore. She was very good at keeping herself on track and doing what was right for her. There had been a time in her life when she did what was right for everyone else.

But not anymore. She had learned that life was too short, too unpredictable to waste.

She placed a hand on her hip and added a cocky tilt to her head. "I should send you away with the muffin and a cup of coffee. But I'm desperate. And yes, I could use the help. If you're sure, then I would say you're on. I can supply all the muffins and coffee that you can eat and drink. And great company." She splayed a hand open toward the ladies, who were back to watching them with expectant expressions.

His lips quirked upward into a dazzling smile that instantly set butterflies doing crazy, amazing aerobatics inside her chest. *Focus, girl.* "Is that a smile of agreement?" she asked.

"Yes. And excitement at getting more of your amazing muffins. I might have to try a few pastries too. Maybe a cupcake."

She laughed. "Of course. The display is yours. And that brings us to some other important issues. Have you ever baked muffins before?"

"Nope, I hate to tell you that I haven't. I'm a fast learner, though. Then again, I have to warn you that I can't imagine anything I could ever mix up would come close to those fantastic muffins you brought me the other day. I loved every delicious bite."

Oh, he was good. She swayed slightly toward him, woozy with delight. "Baking is just science and ingredients. But since we are on a tight timeframe, I will mix and you can pour it into the muffin pans. I'll get you an apron."

"Now that, I can do." He glanced down at her pink apron with the Bake My Day logo scrawled across it and hitched a brow as he looked back at her. "I think for wearing this pink apron…" He lifted it and his brows scrunched over teasing eyes. "I'm going to need a muffin right away. And a cup of coffee."

The man was too adorable. She reminded herself that he was not a puppy but a man, and she was not in the market for a puppy or a man. *But who knew what tomorrow might bring?* She slammed the door on that thought, not certain she would ever be ready for a man like Adam. Instead of letting her thoughts dig her deeper into that hole, she turned toward the glass-enclosed counter. "Ladies, we have recruited some new help. Dr. Sinclair is in the house."

Whoops erupted as she reached into the display full of muffins. Birdie, Lila, Doreen, and Mami clapped as they called out congratulations and thanks. Rosie heard a couple of quiet "I told you so's" pass between them, too.

"I might get in the way more than anything," he warned.

"Not on your worst day," Birdie grunted. "Again, remember, we just like looking at you."

A deep dimple appeared as he laughed, looking slightly uncomfortable, and she thought his cheeks turned a shade of plum beneath his tan.

"I do like a man with dimples," Mami called, then giggled.

Rosie grinned and let the ladies have their fun. "Which would you like?"

Looking grateful to focus on the display, he looked thoughtful. "You did a great job picking the last one, so give me whatever you think I need today."

"Oh, then I have just the muffin for you." She pulled out a double chocolate with a cream cheese center and handed it to him. "Chocolate is a masterful stress reliever and the cream cheese center is a delight to tempt your taste buds into complete bliss." She placed it into his outstretched hand, being careful not to touch him. "One coffee coming right up." She hurried away, putting distance between them while thinking about what touching him did to her. The brief memory of that one brush of his hand on hers had sent her entire body into a heat that made her think she was having a hot flash. And she was way too young to even know what that felt like. And her heart had nearly gone out of rhythm when it practically jumped out of her chest. Yes, it was true: this man did things to her that she didn't quite understand.

But it would be nice to figure it all out.

She wasn't naïve; she knew she was attracted to him. But she had never been attracted to anyone like this and it was scary. *You are no scaredy-cat.*

True. She was a warrior.

She might be a little thing, but she *was* a mighty warrior. She had proved that.

She moved to her beautiful coffeemaker, and with slightly trembling hands produced a cup of bold coffee. She put a lid on it, then returned to him. "I put it in a to-go cup, not because you are leaving but because it's insulated, and your hands are about to be busy so I don't want it to sit in the open mug and get cold. This will keep warm longer as you fill the muffin pans."

He was already halfway through eating the chocolate muffin and he had a little crumb on the side of his mouth. Without thinking, she reached up and dusted it off. "You have a little chocolate—" She froze, realizing she had just dusted the chocolate from his lip. She jerked her hand back and her cheeks heated again. *What—was she living in a sauna now?*

"I'm sorry. What was I thinking?"

He grinned and winked. "That I had chocolate on my lips and I needed it removed." His tone was teasing and flirtatious.

Her heart did crazy things. She was a grown adult and needed to get hold of her runaway reactions to Adam.

You're allowed to flirt with a man.

"Right," she muttered, backing up against the counter. "That's what I was thinking." She spun away, grabbed a measuring cup and dipped it into the tub of flour. Her hand continued to tremble slightly as she dumped the ingredients into the large mixing bowl.

The truth hit her. *I am allowed to flirt. I'm allowed to date. Because I am still alive.*

She was alive…she had beaten the odds.

She was twenty-five years old and she had her whole life ahead of her, which hadn't been the case less than a year ago. Not only could she date if she wanted to, but now she could dream of finding her happily-ever-after. She paused, scooping flour into the mixing bowl as the thought settled over her. In her very recent past, she couldn't do any of that because her life had an expiration date on it.

She'd had to focus all her energy on overcoming her date with death.

And praise God, she had.

And now, she could do what normal young women her age did and that was look to her future. Which she was doing. But, as the voice in her head sternly reminded her, that also meant her future with a husband and a family. That was the scary part—and as hard as it was for her to admit it…it was true.

Despite the fact that she was a warrior, she wasn't sure she was ready to face this part of her life. It was all so confusing. And it meant the next several hours were going to be very awkward if she was unable to get control of her runaway reactions to Doctor Adam Sinclair.

CHAPTER FIVE

Adam wasn't sure how he'd ended up in this situation. He had come into the bakery for a muffin and ended up in over his head with the beautiful muffin maker. *And* the four ladies at the table giving him not-so-hidden stares as they watched him and Rosie behind the counter. The fact that they'd told him they liked his dimples and they liked looking at him…made the entire situation a little uncomfortable. Not that he wasn't a bit used to older ladies acting a little bit eccentric at times. But these ladies were just having fun; they were just teasing and he knew it. It was the fact that they were watching him and Rosie together that made him uncomfortable. Did they see the sparks flying between them like sparklers on the Fourth of July?

He'd almost kissed her. Still wanted to. And for him, that was the first feelings of being alive inside that he'd felt in months.

He hadn't come in here expecting to help her behind the counter, but he was glad he was. She intrigued him now more than ever. He wanted to know her story.

He stared at the back of her neck, exposed because her hair was pulled up into a ponytail, and he had the sudden desire to walk over and kiss the soft spot behind her ear. She turned to him suddenly, catching him staring, and all he could do was smile and probably look completely guilty about what he'd been crazily contemplating.

Her eyes narrowed. "You're not working. Maybe I need to show you what you need to be doing now. Here, this batch is ready. Let's start putting them in the muffin tins."

"Sure, show me. I'm at your disposal."

Looking flustered, she grabbed the bowl, the very big bowl, and carried it over to a table where there were several large muffin pans on a counter beside a rack with several shelves.

"This container will fill six of these muffin pans."

"It's a pretty color," he said, thinking the soft pink of the batter matched her pretty lips.

"These are my cherry crunch muffins. You'll take this." She picked up an ice cream scoop, snapped the button on the side a couple of times—he assumed to show him how the scoop worked—then she dipped it into the mix and carefully held it over the muffin pans. "Just squeeze the button and let the batter drop into place. One scoop per muffin. When the pan is full, place it on the rack and I'll start putting them in the oven as we go. We'll get a system going and have this place smelling like heaven in just a little bit."

He was all too aware of how close they were standing and that was pretty close to heaven to him. She caught him staring again. He added quickly, "It already does. I don't know how you stay here all day. I would be eating everything in sight just because it smelled so good."

She laughed—a little breathlessly, he thought—as she moved a step away from him.

"I resist. Besides, I have eaten a lot of this over and over again, so the newness has worn off."

"What you're saying is you don't eat your own stuff."

"No, I'm not saying that. I just don't eat as much as my customers do because a lot of a good thing is a bad thing. A little of a good thing is a good thing. You understand?"

He chuckled, enjoying watching her. "I know what you mean." He got the uncanny feeling that he'd never get tired of watching her. She was a good thing. A very good thing.

"Doc Sinclair," Mami called, drawing his attention. "You look like you could eat anything you wanted to."

"I so agree," Lila said, smiling. "Do you jog? You know, to keep your physique so perfect?"

Birdie harrumphed. "It is perfect. I saw it the other

day when I went by with paperwork. He was just coming up from a dip in the ocean. Yep, pretty perfect."

From the corner of his vision, he saw Rosie's shoulder shaking. He glanced at her and she batted her big eyes at him, a mock attempt at looking innocent.

"Well, do you, Doc Sinclair?" Rosie drawled, lightly.

His lips twitched. "Yes ma'am, I do jog."

"Oh, I knew it," Lila declared. "I just love a man who runs."

"I do too," Mami agreed.

Rosie laughed, enjoying the show.

"I always wanted to jog," Doreen grunted. "But my assets always got in the way." She looked down at her "assets," which were causing her to sit farther back from the table than the other ladies.

"I never had that problem." Birdie laughed, looking down at her fairly flat chest.

Lila's eyes were wide. "Mine get in my way sometimes, though not like yours, Doreen."

"Ladies, there is a gentleman in the room," Mami

scolded.

"He's a *doctor.*" Birdie laughed as giggles erupted around the table.

He looked to Rosie for help. She was biting her lip as her face turned red and her eyes watered. The woman was fighting near hysteria as she looked at him.

"Am I turning red?" he groaned.

"Like a beet." She placed her hand on his forearm. "They've never been so bad before. It's like you bring the naughty out in them. I don't know what's going on, but obviously they like you."

"Gee, I'm so lucky."

"Actually, yes. They're adorable, lovely ladies. And they don't like everybody."

He glanced over at the ladies and they were all grinning widely.

Doreen looked a little bit mortified. "I can't believe I said that. I don't often talk like that. Lila does, but not me."

Lila gasped. "I do not talk about my boobs in front of people."

"Yes, you do," Mami challenged.

"Don't be embarrassed, Doreen," Birdie said. "Again, may I remind you he is a doctor. I'm sure he's heard and seen it all."

"That's true," the pink-faced Doreen said, looking relieved. "I thought about having them, you know, reduced. But I was a chicken and so I didn't and can't jog, but I envy those who do."

He fought to keep a straight face. "Well, there are other ways to exercise besides jogging. Yoga is good."

"I love yoga," Lila said. "You should come with me."

Doreen looked pointedly at her friend. "I went with you once and it was a disaster. I bent forward to do that forward dog move, or whatever it's called, and I toppled over like a top-heavy ostrich egg. My balance was not too good. I'll just stick to walking. Walking and I get along just fine."

"Me too," Mami said. "When you walk, you get to see all those good-looking men jogging. So, it's the best of all worlds."

"Is that why you walk something like twelve miles

a day?" Birdie asked Mami.

"I don't walk twelve miles a day."

"Seems like it," Birdie snapped.

"Maybe you all should take up walking with me," Mami said. "It is very entertaining and then we could always come back here and end the morning with another muffin."

"Ladies." Lila sighed. "We better change the subject. The preacher's going to come in and hear us talking like this and kick us out of the church. He'll think we're *wild* women or something." She chuckled.

Birdie looked insulted. "Just because I go over there to the Bayside Church every Sunday morning doesn't mean I'm blind and can't have some fun. Why, I'll have you know—"

"Ladies—" Rosie interrupted Birdie's growing indignation. "Why don't we change the subject and talk about the festival tomorrow. That is what we are getting ready for."

"I think the festival will be great," Adam said, more than glad to help get the ladies talking about something other than boobs.

"Will we see you at the festival tomorrow?" Rosie asked, a spark of interest in her eyes.

"I had thought about it, but I'm thinking about going fishing instead."

"Fishing," Birdie grunted. "Is that all you do?"

He wasn't sure what to think about her accusatory tone. "Well, not all I do. I'm working on the bungalow. I'm helping Doc Coleman two days a week. And yes, now that I'm back in town, I'm enjoying some fishing and also hoping to get back to doing a little surfing when the waves perk up a little bit. And today I'm helping Rosie with these muffins." He wasn't sure whether hanging out around Rosie tomorrow was a good idea. He was thinking too strongly about nearly kissing her earlier and the interest he'd just seen in her eyes had rekindled the flame he felt.

"You surf?" Mami called. "I just love seeing a man get out there and ride that wave on that board."

Here they went again.

"Ohhh, I do too," Lila said.

"Ladies, halt," Rosie said, smiling at him. "I think surfing is pretty cool too, but I've never had much luck. The few times I tried, it was disastrous. Anyway, back to talking about the festival."

"What happened?" he asked, curious about what had happened to her surfing.

"I drank a lot of water. Choked a good bit. It was not pretty. I almost killed myself on the last try. It really scared me."

He could tell by the tone of her words that she was serious. "Maybe we'll have to try to overcome that unfortunate impression."

"I bet he's a good teacher, Rosie," Mami called.

"If I was twenty years younger, I'd have you teach me," Lila said, wishfully.

"What do you mean, twenty? You mean thirty, don't you?" Birdie laughed and Lila slapped her arm.

"I'd sink the minute I waded past the four-foot mark and flip right over like a cork, with my feet sticking out of the water." Doreen gave a heavy sigh and then giggled, and Adam had to fight not chuckling at the picture she'd just painted.

"Thank you, ladies, for your confidence in my abilities. It's been awhile since I surfed consistently, so

I'm still getting my feet back under me. I would like to help you, though," he said to Rosie again.

"It fits you better than just painting and fishing all the time. I look at you and just think that you were not an avid fisherman."

"No, I'm not an avid fisherman. It's not like I eat, breathe, and talk about it all the time. No, I like other things. So back to your question about my coming to the festival—do you need help tomorrow?"

"Oh yes, she does," Birdie called. "You gonna rescue her? That would be wonderful. She really needs it. She's gonna be so swamped tomorrow at that festival that she's not going to know what to do. Her head is going to be spinning. Yes, she needs help."

"Birdie," Rosie called.

"Don't Birdie me—you know it's true."

Mami said, "We're going to try to help her, but we have commitments to other committees. And, well, to be honest, we would love it more if you would help her. I just think it'd be cute. You two, looking good over there at the muffin stand. Maybe think about opening up a kissing booth?"

CHAPTER SIX

By the time they had made what Adam thought was enough muffins to supply the entire state of Florida, he and Rosie walked out of the bakery and she locked the door behind them. The ladies had finished everything they needed to do a couple of hours earlier and gone home. They were nice—a little scary, but nice. But, to be honest, he had not minded that they left and he and Rosie had a few hours to be alone. Not that they talked about anything important. A lot of the time they worked in silence, but it had been pleasant and that hum of attraction that was between them kept right on making its music. He wasn't sure he was going to act on that attraction, but he still enjoyed it. Enjoyed the possibility that he wasn't completely dead inside. Because until he met Rosie, he'd begun to think that he might be.

"Okay, we're going to load your bicycle in the back of my truck and I'm giving you a ride home. Then, in the morning—however bright and early you need me to get up—I'll load you up and I'll bring you back here. I'll help you take those muffins, however you plan to get them down there to your booth, and I'll help you set up and, as planned, stick around to help. Deal?"

She turned toward him after locking the door. She was actually tired. She had been on her feet all day long, since she'd started at four in the morning. He didn't start that early, although he didn't sleep well at night.

"If you're sure, I really could use the help. But my goodness, you're the doctor in town. I mean, you don't have to help me sell muffins. And coffee."

"Did you see how many of those muffins I ate

tonight? I plan on eating just that many more, too, as I hand them out. Everybody else gives you money for it. Besides, I have a feeling that if I don't show up tomorrow, those four ladies are going to come after me."

"You might be right about that. Although I would tell them to go easy on you, you know—because you're a nice guy and my neighbor and all."

"Why, that would be generous of you." They walked toward his truck. On the way, he picked her bike up from where it was against the rail and carried it. He lifted it and put it in the back of the truck. He was on his way around to open the door for her but she already had it opened.

"I would have done that for you."

"Do I look like I need you to open the door for me?"

He expected that from her. "No, you look plenty strong enough to open your own door, despite being about as big as a kitten. But you gotta be tired and, well, I like to open doors."

"Well, thanks. Maybe next time." She laughed and

hopped up into the seat, winking at him as she pulled the door closed.

He stood there and stared in the window at her, then went to get in on his side. "You're very independent."

She looked thoughtful and nodded. "I enjoy being independent. Like I told you, I came here and started my bakery. I enjoy it and I like that I'm doing it on my own. I like that it's mine. I do like my independence." She paused. "I can't thank you enough for helping me, and I would very much appreciate the lift to my shop in the morning and then your help setting up. After all, it will give Birdie and the other ladies a chance to see you again. You know, maybe you could wear a tank top or something—something to show your muscles off. Maybe you can flex them—get a lot of people coming over for a muffin or something."

He looked at her and frowned. "Tell me you're joking."

She giggled. He really liked her giggle. "Of course, I'm joking. I have no idea whether your muscles would draw people over to eat muffins or not."

He laughed at that. "You got me. And you're right—they probably wouldn't."

"I don't know. Those biceps were flexing pretty good when you were making muffins in there."

She was funny, that was for sure. "How can you be this energetic? It's like one a.m. Given you've been up since what—four?"

"Yeah." She sighed. "Probably before that. As I get tired, I'm a little bit giddy and a little bit loopy. You know, I'll probably fall on the bed with all my clothes on and just pass out. You'll probably have to bang on my door in the morning and wake me up."

"So you're always this funny when you're this tired?"

She smiled sweetly as he pulled into the drive. "I don't know if I'd call it funny, but I guess I do get a little bit silly."

"I like it. It's good to not always be serious or worry so much about what people think, and that you can have a little fun. Keeps you healthy."

And it was such a relief from where he'd been

before he came here. He needed something to help him not be so serious. But when you were dealing with life-and-death issues and people in anguish, it was hard to keep your head above water sometimes.

"Where'd you go?"

"Excuse me?"

She was studying him as he turned the key and cut the engine. "You were just kind of staring out there, watching the ocean. We were in park for a couple seconds. You thinking hard about something? And I noticed you sometimes, when I've gotten up late, sitting on the porch. You keep odd hours, you know."

He wasn't sure what to say. "I didn't know you looked out your window. But yeah, I have trouble sleeping sometimes." He felt self-conscious thinking about her seeing him when he was feeling lost and confused. But looking at her, he wasn't feeling lost at that moment.

"I'm sorry you have so much trouble sleeping."

"Thanks. One day it will get better, I hope."

"Me too."

They stared at each other in the dim light of the

dashboard. He was reluctant to get out of the truck, reluctant to tell her goodnight. "I had a...good time this evening. Even with getting harassed by the ladies."

"I can see you grinning in the dark. You made Birdie and Lila and the other ladies' evening. They were just going to be stuck with me in there all evening, boring old me and boring themselves dipping those muffins in that chocolate. But then you walked in and boy did you give them something to talk about."

He was grinning big now. "You enjoyed that, didn't you? You enjoyed watching them give me a hard time."

"I cannot deny what is the truth. It's not often you see a handsome doctor dimple up and blush."

He wasn't too sure he liked the sound of what she just said. It didn't really sound flattering. "Dimple up and blush—well, what a description." Not exactly masculine, either.

She giggled. "I can't help it. You do have some dimples. Speaking of which, do your other family members have dimples?"

"One of my brothers does and so does one of my

sisters."

"Tell me again how many you have—three brothers and two sisters?"

"Yes, so there's six of us."

"Big family."

"Pretty big. I just came back from Windswept Bay—you know, across the bay a bit there—I have cousins living up there. That's a big family, with nine brothers and sisters."

"A very big family. Still, six—that's a good size."

"And then we had at least three friends who were practically in our house all the time, who are just like brothers. I'm sure you've met some of them at some point in time. My brother was here a few days ago and he actually told me about your coffee shop—told me I need to stop in and that he enjoys it. He looks a lot like me. I'm surprised when you saw me, you didn't think I was him."

"I see a lot of people coming in the bakery and if I have met him, I just can't place him at the moment. Maybe he was only there one time or maybe he was there when I had helpers working. I do take some time off once in a while. Although I am a control freak and I try to do most of the baking myself."

"Yeah, I get that, too. And understand it. I mean, you're really good at what you do and I don't care how many times you tell me that baking is all about science and ingredients—you put something in that stuff that nobody else can put in there." She smiled at that and he felt the tight knot that was ever-present in his chest ease a little.

Adam's words settled around Rosie and a flutter of butterflies rose through her chest. The silence of the late-night settled around them and she opened the door and got out of the truck. He did the same as they headed toward her house she let his words sink in.

It was a wonderful evening, with the sound of the surf gently rolling in as the bright moon beamed an endless trail on the open water. The recent full moon gave her an easy view of Adam. She was very aware of how romantic a night it was, and if she let herself be honest, she could very easily give in to the romantic part of it. The connection that tugged between them like a tightening rope kept drawing her toward him. Her arm brushed his as they walked and her stomach clenched tight. Something about him made her feel that she would be safe with him. That her secrets would be safe and so would her emotions. That if she shared what she'd been through, it would be okay.

But she wouldn't.

Because despite what her gut was telling her, there was still that doubt, that worry that revealing her life before moving to Sunset Bay left her open and vulnerable, and that was one thing keeping her secrets protected. Right now, she was not vulnerable. She was strong and invincible. She was a go-getter, getting what she wanted, doing what she wanted, making herself and others happy with her baked goods and good deeds. And she was doing it with confidence and vigor, and that was partly because no one reminded her of how far she'd come. Of how weak and helpless she had been.

She didn't completely understand the feelings that she was having or why she didn't want people to know her story. Back home, people had looked at her with pity and most of them hadn't really believed she could overcome. She understood, but it hadn't helped her. Hadn't bolstered her spirits to fight for her life. She'd done that on her own, with the help of her doctor and her faith and her belief that she could.

Maybe keeping her past in the past was because she needed distance from that terminal patient she had been, who had no hope…she needed distance from that right now. She had been there but she wasn't now. She was looking forward. If she told any of the people around her in her new home of Sunset Bay, then they would have the perspective of looking back on where she'd been and where she was now. Some might think that was a good thing. Some might say they liked what she'd accomplished—for what she overcame; her story was inspiring and her story could help others. That could be true, but she would rather look at it like she was inspiring people now without them knowing where she'd been.

And so she didn't tell him and she didn't get into the feeling that had her wanting to walk over, wrap her arms around his waist and lay her head on his strong chest. Because she did want to see that; she wanted to feel his heartbeat beating against her ear, wanted to feel the strong muscles of his back against her hands as she wrapped her arms around him. She wanted to feel the brush of his lips against her temple, against her eyelids, ending on her lips. She wanted to feel that. She wanted what so many people took for granted and she had never had. It wasn't easy being twenty-five and never been kissed. But that was her. Hard to believe now with the person that she was. People would look at her and just assume that she dated all of her life. They didn't realize that the person that she had been was too shy to be kissed and then too sick to be kissed and now too busy and too focused to be kissed.

Standing here on the moonlit beach of the beautiful ocean, she wished her neighbor—her new friend —would kiss her. She wished even though her heart and her mind told her that if she got what she wished for, she might not be able to handle it.

So what was a girl to do? "You know, I think you might be right about me and that baking thing, because when I bake—muffins or pastries or cakes or pies—I want so much for what I bake or the coffee I brew to make someone happy, to brighten their day and to make them smile because of the flavor that bursts in their mouth when they bite into something that I created. Much as the name of my bakery says, I want to bake someone's day beautiful. 'Bake my day' is my attempt to make my day, and yes, that connotation came from a movie so long ago that was more about mindless violence. But this is my twist on it and it's a good thing—it's not a bad thing. I really want to bake something that makes someone feel special, to make someone's day beautiful." It sounded kind of silly sometimes to think that she believed baked goods could be something like that, but Rosie believed that everyone had the power of passing on something nice, that a small something could make the difference. Big things started with little things—even a muffin baked to perfection.

"That's exactly what I think it is," Adam said. "I didn't know exactly how you would describe it, but now I think you're just what the doctor ordered. I think that if I were seeing some of my patients, that I'd be singing your praises—that if I saw someone and they were having a bad day, I would say why don't you go by Bake My Day and get a cherry muffin or orange muffin or any muffin that delights you, and if you like a cup of coffee with caffeine or one of those other concoctions you make that are low-calorie. I would say grab one of those and then head to this beautiful beach and sit down or stroll along this beach as you eat and drink and enjoy. I think that would be a good thing for the doctor to order—it would help with blood pressure and then if they ate in moderation, it would be okay—unless they're diabetic. Are you making things that diabetics can eat?"

"Oh yes, I've started baking some of my muffins with monk fruit, a sweetener that doesn't raise your blood sugar. So, yes, I even make that for diabetics or others who just don't need sugar, which would be most people. But you can't convince everybody, you know."

"I know, definitely. You know, working the trauma unit, it was so sad that I saw people who had more gunshot wounds and things like that than I did people who were overweight and needed to lose weight or had low blood sugar or high blood sugar—diabetes. Yeah, I saw seizures and you know, people going into shock from things like that, but it wasn't often that I told someone that they needed to change their diet in order to feel healthy. Mostly I pulled the bullet out of somebody…" He paused and looked out at the scene.

She wondered suddenly whether this was what was bothering him. This peek into his life as a trauma doctor sounded rather depressing.

"Do you think working and seeing so much trauma from violence—did that get to you? Or, now that I think about it, you probably worked a lot of car accidents, too, and I'm guessing that maybe a lot of that was from drunk drivers? Things that could be prevented or seemed senseless. Did you see things along that line?"

He turned to stare at her as if seeing her for the first time. His expression was troubled. And she knew right then that she had hit the target of what she had been feeling from him—that something wasn't right.

She wondered whether this was what drove him to sit on his porch at all hours of the night.

"You're right. I saw a lot of senseless, terrible things that could have been prevented. If people just didn't drink so much, or had a designated driver, or just hadn't gotten on the road... Innocent families—innocent children—through no fault of their own are being harmed by senseless acts of someone else, whether a drunk driver or someone texting—just senseless things. A drug sell gone bad. Drug overdoses. It all got to me—"

Unable to stop herself, she placed her hand on his arm, felt his muscles tense and she squeezed gently. "I can tell you that I agree that life is full of things we don't understand—illness, violence. I know in my heart that this world is full of trouble. I also know that it's full of beauty, too, and if you let the ugly steal the joy and the beauty, that's very sad. I'm glad you're here. I'm sure your family is glad you're here. I know Doctor Coleman's glad you're here and I know that all of his patients who see you will be glad that you're here. You have skills, I'm quite sure.

"I'm so glad you're going to help me tomorrow. I think it'll be good to see our little town and how cool it is. People are going to turn out. They're going to be smiling about muffins and going to buy all kinds of stuff up and down the street. And they're going to enjoy the music. It's just going to be the best of small-town living. I think it would be good for you. Because I know that while you've been here, you've pretty much been a recluse. So getting out and about will be good. I can pay you—I am grateful for your help. And I promise I haven't been spying on you." She thought of the blonde.

"Hey, it's your kitchen window. You have a right to look out of it. And you're right. I haven't had many visitors. One of my sisters came by and a couple of my brothers have dropped over briefly. Other than that I've stayed close to home working. Going to the office has gotten me out some. And hanging out at your shop and interacting with the ladies and you—that's probably about the most I have been out there."

"Is your sister blonde?" She had to know.

His lip hitched and his dimple dug in on one

cheek. "She is. You've put that window to good use."

She cringed. "Like you said, it's my window."

He laughed. "Yes it is. So, my peeping Rosie, it will be good to be out and about tomorrow and to check out the community. I remember the festival from when I was younger and it was always fun. I'm going to let you go inside now because it won't be long before the crack of dawn hits and I'm banging on your door to wake you."

"That sounds like a great plan. Even the banging on my door, because I am wiped out—so tired, I may want to sleep till noon tomorrow. That can't happen, not after all the work we've done. Besides that, after all the work that Birdie and the other ladies did, they would come down to bang on our doors and get us both up and we'd both be in trouble. So I'm going to set my alarm—you set your alarm and we'll be backup for each other."

He grinned. "I'll be your backup anytime." He turned to go and then turned back. "Oh, thanks. I haven't talked much about what was going on with me while at the trauma unit until now. Actually, I talked a little bit once to my cousins, who had some issues after they got out of the military, and I knew they would understand. I talked with them and they talked with me, and that was helpful. My family didn't know, so I hope that you keep it to yourself."

"Of course I will. I'd never even dream of speaking of it other than to you. I understand more than you know. Goodnight, Adam." She turned, walked up her steps, and opened the door. She turned and looked back. He was still watching her. She waved her fingers at him and then closed the door behind her.

She was in trouble and she knew it. That something about him that drew her in just got stronger. And she wasn't sure she wanted to resist it.

CHAPTER SEVEN

When Sunset Bay had a festival, they had a festival. Adam and Rosie unloaded early at her booth and had barely gotten everything set up before people began to arrive. He soon realized that Rosie's muffins were going to be the big seller of the entire festival. They couldn't even keep them stocked fast enough.

He kept having to pull box after box from beneath the table where they were stashed. He kept thinking the day before when they'd filled those large boxes with muffins that there was no way they'd sell them all...

He had been wrong. It wasn't noon yet and they were two-thirds of the way sold. He felt as if he'd been in the trauma unit, where he was used to moving fast. People here acted as though he were saving their lives when they came up, almost desperate to get one of Rosie's treats before they were all gone. It was crazy. It was so different than what he was used to doing that it was a welcomed feeling. He was enjoying himself.

During the day Rosie was handing out cards left and right, and smiles right along with them. He hadn't eaten a muffin today, deciding he'd better let the customers have them; besides, he knew where the bakery was and planned to frequent it often. And it wasn't because of her orange spice blueberry twist muffins or her cinnamon pumpkin cranberry explosions. It was because of her, the woman.

He'd never seen anything like Rosie Olsen. She was like a daisy in a desert. She was just happy and smiling and...joyous. She greeted the hordes of people with a delighted exclamation. There was nothing fake about the woman. She absolutely was thrilled with each person who approached her table.

And he delighted in watching her.

He was halfway through the morning when he realized the truth. He had not just burned out from his job, but had become disillusioned, jaded. Where had his humanity gone? Yes, in the trauma unit he saw car wrecks, shootings, and all manner of injuries from violence. He'd signed on for it, thrived on saving lives, but somewhere along the way, he'd become angry seeing so much pain and anguish that should never have happened in the first place.

Watching Rosie in action, there was no room for anger. There was something really special about her and he was like a thirsty man from a desert.

She didn't always have time when there was a line waiting, but still she tried to make each person feel special. When there was someone who seemed alone or dejected, she gave them an extra moment of her time and gave them a little extra special gift of love. That's what it was, he realized, she seemed to be spreading love and her delicious muffins were the vehicle she used to do it. She was her own secret ingredient.

He had decided, watching her, that at some point in her life or her career, Rosie had decided to be an investor of love and she was doing it through her bakery in her outreach. His heart cracked open watching her, as if the window to his jaded opinions opened and the fresh air of her mission blew in through the crack and filled him. He wanted to know everything there was to know about her, especially what drove her. Because he decided that she was driven; she worked too hard at it not to be. What was her story? He hadn't been this curious about a woman in a very long time. Maybe ever. Something about her called to him.

"Hey, Adam, what's up?" Brad stood on the other side of the table, hands on his hips, grinning at him. "Are you in the muffin business now?"

Adam laughed, glad to see his brother. "I am for the day. Rosie, the owner, is my neighbor. I stopped by the bakery, not realizing she owned it, and ended up getting roped into helping her and a few of her customers get ready for the day. Since I was off today I came to help."

"Really. What customers?"

"Do you know Birdie Carmichael? I bought the cottage from her. And her friends Mami—"

Brad chuckled, while nodding. "I know Birdie and Mami, *and* Lila. I know exactly how you got roped into it now. Doreen was probably involved too, but she's quiet and not one to instigate."

He thought of Doreen and how shy she seemed. "I see you're taking your job pretty seriously, Fire Chief. You know your community."

Brad looked suddenly serious. "Yeah, I do. I try to know everyone, but those ladies are always at all of the firehouse fund drives. Everybody knows them. They get involved. You'll see as the doc in town that they're always there to help out if you need something."

"Good to know. Did you stop by for a muffin or to see me?"

"Are you kidding? I'm here for muffins. Rosie dropped a batch of them by the firehouse last week and I'm hooked."

"Hi." Rosie came over, smiling. "You're the fire chief."

"And my brother," Adam said.

"I'm glad you remembered. I'm going to get another dozen muffins. A couple for me and then I'll drop them off at the firehouse for the guys. They loved them."

"I am so glad. And I heard the girls talking about you being brothers last night when Adam was helping bake muffins."

Brad's expression changed to open curiosity. "My brother helped you bake muffins last night?"

Rosie looked from him to his brother. "Ummm, yes. He did a very good job."

Brad crossed his arms over his chest and grinned. "When you said you helped, I had no idea you meant you baked. Wow."

Adam laughed, knowing full well that he would never hear the end of this.

"He was a little rusty at first but he's a fast learner."

"I'm sure he is."

Adam shot Brad a warning. "Lay off the teasing. I'll get your muffins and then you'd better move out of the way and let someone else move up in line."

"Hey, you trying to get rid of me?"

Adam made no move to sugarcoat his answer. "Yes I am."

Brad's eyes twinkled. "Fine. Totally understandable."

More people moved into the other line and Rosie smiled. "Enjoy the muffins," she said and went to take orders.

"Of course. They're the best," Brad called to her.

Adam watched Rosie welcome the new customers with her big smile then he handed Brad a full bag and tore his gaze off of her to look at his brother. Brad was smiling broadly at him and Adam realized he might have lingered too long on Rosie.

"Your neighbor," Brad said with a bit too much interest. "That's cozy. Mom is going to be over the moon when she finds out about this."

"Hold it, swear to me you are not mentioning this to Mom."

Brad looked innocent. "Why wouldn't I tell her?"

"Because, I'm just helping out and Mom might get

the wrong idea."

Brad laughed. "I'm just teasing. I totally get it and she won't hear it from me. But believe me, she'll hear it from someone."

Adam knew she would and he would never hear the end of it.

Rosie was amazed all day at how supportive and helpful Adam had been. He was a real trooper. She hadn't expected him to stick around the entire day but he did, and he'd watched intently as she worked, as if he were figuring her out, detail by detail. She wanted to know his story, too.

She kept thinking about last night, outside their cottages. She'd been so drawn to him, and more so now. Every moment around him drew her to wanting more time with him. He was so kind to everyone who came by the booth and she could tell his bedside manner as a doctor would be wonderful. His patients had to love him.

When she had been so ill, a doctor or nurse's

attitude could help brighten her day.

"He's a doll, isn't he?" Birdie startled Rosie out of her deep thoughts.

"Um, yes, he is."

"We've been watching, but because the two of you were so busy we didn't want to come over till now." Birdie grinned. "You two work well together. Had a happy crowd all day. I've been waiting on a muffin all day long. Had to settle for a funnel cake for breakfast."

"For breakfast?" Adam asked, looking skeptical.

Rosie thought she was seeing his doctor face and she had to smile.

"Hey, it's no worse than a donut."

"True, but who said a donut was healthy?"

"True, but it sure was good. I'd have felt better with the muffin, though. At least I know Rosie puts good ingredients in them."

Rosie knew even her muffins weren't good if they were eaten in excess, but still, her heart warmed at Birdie's kind words.

"Speaking of which, I'll take an orange

marmalade zest." Birdie winked.

"And I'll have a raspberry delight," Mami called, hustling across the street. "I thought I was never going to get loose to come by."

"Us too," Lila called, with Doreen huffing along behind her. When Lila reached them, she pushed her glasses back up the bridge of her nose and grinned. "It's muffin time."

Doreen leaned on the table, heaving deep breaths. "I thought you might be out. Lila, you didn't have to practically run. I'm all tuckered out now."

Lila looked pointedly at her friend. "Yoga. I already told you that you need to join the class."

"Do not go there today, please." Doreen scowled at her, breathlessly.

"Ladies, it's good you're here and muffins are coming right up." Rosie smiled as she reached for a muffin at the same time Adam reached for the same one. Their hands met and their gazes locked.

"Allow me," he said, showing a dimple.

Her insides fluttered. The man looked better than a muffin any day. She let go of the muffin and tried not to appear too flustered.

"Such a gentleman," Mami cooed.

"Isn't he." Lila batted her eyes at him.

It was easy to see he had an effect on all ladies, not just her.

"You are one efficient helper, Doctor Sinclair," Birdie said, eyeing them both with avid speculation. "You're just the man Rosie needed today."

"I had to stay on my toes all day. I think the only reason we're having a little slack time right now is people ate lunch and are full."

"I think you're right. But they'll be coming for round two soon."

Doreen nodded. "It's a wonder if you make it to four o'clock, though. Y'all have to be about out."

"They are," Birdie said. "I never dreamed you would go through all we made yesterday. As good as your stuff is, I never dreamed they'd fly away like that."

"We ran out of muffin balls about an hour ago," Rosie said as Adam handed out the muffins.

"No charge, ladies. Thank you so much. And

tomorrow, coffee and muffins are on the house." Rosie felt Adam step near her, felt the heat off his body, and her skin warmed. She enjoyed him being here with her.

"Speaking of lunch," he said. "I'll go find us something to eat, if you can hold the fort down while I'm gone?"

"That sounds wonderful. I am getting a little bit hungry. And if it goes as fast and furious as it did this morning, we'll need some sustenance for the afternoon." She felt the looks from the ladies as they watched them closely. She was sure they'd noticed her reaction when she'd grabbed his hand.

"You are a sweetheart, aren't you?" Mami said.

Birdie stopped eating long enough to add, "You know, there's a guy down there that's making a roasted chicken on a stick and it is delicious. And kinda healthy since you look like you're thinking health-wise. I figure you'd look on a corndog with about as much affection as you had for my funnel cake."

"He doesn't like funnel cakes? Oh dear, they're wonderful," Lila added.

"The corndogs are on an open pit—they aren't

fried," Mami said, trying to justify the corndogs. "I think you would like them. And he also makes French fries that are very tasty..." Mami frowned. "Not that I've eaten any today. Because they would really mess up my diet. I saved that for the muffins."

"I ate the fries and corndog," Doreen said softly and grimaced. "Maybe I shouldn't have but I just couldn't help myself."

Adam patted her shoulder. "It's okay, ladies. Relax. I'm not the food police, so just forget I'm a doctor and enjoy your day. If the chicken sounds good to you, Rosie, I think that's what I'll get."

"Go for it." Rosie didn't care what she ate as long as he came back and spent the rest of the day with her.

"Then I'll be back soon. Don't have too much fun while I'm gone. I feel like I'll be missing out."

They laughed and watched him leave. Rosie couldn't help but stare.

"He's a good fella," Birdie said. "I think you like him."

"I do too," Lila said and the others echoed her.

"What's not to like?" Mami asked. "And he is so

nice, too, and he can't take his eyes off our Rosie."

Rosie rolled her eyes. "Girls, don't get any ideas. Yes, you're right on all counts but we're just friends. I don't want to rush into anything. Especially relationships."

"Ha," Lila said. "Honey, you better latch onto him now before some of these ladies who hovered around this table get their claws into him. I hate to say it but I don't think you sold all these muffins today purely on their delicious merits. I do believe several of the ladies came back for seconds and thirds."

Rosie hadn't thought of that because she'd been so busy, but now that she did, she could see the truth. She glanced after Adam and caught a flash of red out of the corner of her eye. She focused and saw Lulu Raintree duck behind the Korney Korn trailer, then peek back around the corner. What was she doing?

"Oh dear," Doreen said, drawing Rosie's attention back to see worry on her darling face. "What are you going to do, Rosie? You don't want to lose him."

Sweet lady, Rosie thought. Problem was, she never had him in the first place and wasn't sure what to do with him, even if she wanted him.

"Now all of you need to stop this. I know what you're doing and hoping for, but I have a business to run. I don't have time for romance right now. Someday, but just not right now." When *she* was ready and not before.

"Well, I want to see you have some wedding bells in your future," Mamie said. And of course, everyone echoed her thoughts.

"Right now, the only wedding bells I'm thinking about are Clarence and Belva's. Is everything a go for that?" She glanced back across the street at the Korney Korn trailer and there was that brilliant red head peeking out. Lulu was hiding. But why? Rosie scanned the area. There were people everywhere, but it looked like she was staring at the group of firemen handing out candy on the corner. Brad had stopped to talk to them and was still holding the pink Bake My Day bag in his hand. The big handsome fire chief looked cute holding the pink bag.

"The Sandy Shores is all set," Mami said. "Rosie, are you listening?"

Rosie looked at Mami. "Yes, I am."

"Good. We've lined up the music and the preacher

will be there too. I'll come by and pick you up that morning."

"That sounds good. I'll have Gigi drop the cake off that morning before she opens up and then you and I can get there before the wedding and make sure everything looks great."

"I think it is wonderful you're helping with this wedding," Lila gushed. "I love when older couples get married. Just because a person is over eighty does not mean they can't have a happily-ever-after."

Birdie harrumphed. "I guess," she grunted. "But I'm so set in my ways already that I know at eighty I'll be as set as concrete."

"I think it's lovely," Doreen said. "Everyone should just do what feels right to them. If they want to marry that late in life then so be it. I wish them well. I wish I could be there to celebrate with them and help out, but I'll be out of town."

"It's okay, we've got it handled," Mami said.

Rosie chanced a look back at the Korney Korn trailer but Lulu was gone. What had she been doing? The firemen had moved on down the street too, the crowd parting as the group walked back toward the firehouse, continuing to hand out candy as they went. She was going to have to ask Lulu why in the world she'd been hiding behind the trailer. But now, she needed to pay attention. "Yes, don't worry, we've got this handled."

"We have confidence in you two. I can't be there either." Lila nibbled on her raspberry muffin. "You better wear your dancing shoes, those fellas at the Sandy Shores love to dance."

Mami grinned wide. "I do too, so I'm all set. How about you, Rosie? Do you like to dance?"

"Well, I haven't done that much of it lately, but I'm sure I can follow along." Her gaze went to the throng of people wandering about the street, and this time she saw Adam in the distance. She wondered if he liked to dance. He was probably a great dancer since he was very athletic. Maybe she should ask him…then again, maybe not. He had already spent one of his days here and she knew he had plans of his own. No, she couldn't bother him with that.

But still, the thought of dancing with him was a nice idea.

An idea that she would keep to herself for now.

CHAPTER EIGHT

On Tuesday after the festival, Adam was at his parents' home for dinner with the family. He had come prepared to avoid all questions about why he'd given up his career. He knew his parents were more than curious, but so far had held back and not badgered him for why he would suddenly drop the career he'd worked his life off for. They deserved answers, but he simply hadn't been ready to talk about it with anyone.

The moment he walked into the house, his mother threw her arms around him and hugged him as if he were going to disappear at any moment. When she finally let him loose, she cupped his cheeks between her hands and studied his face as if she hadn't already seen him a couple of times since he'd moved back to town.

"Mom?" he said, smiling.

"It's just so good to see your face again." She patted his cheek affectionately, then let him go. "I just can't tell you how happy I am you are home. I know I'm driving you crazy, but you were so busy with your career and never came home." Her words trailed off and then she took a breath. "I'm going to stop now. I am just so glad to have you so close. How are you doing? Did you enjoy the festival?" She picked up her knife and went back to chopping tomatoes.

"I'm fine. And I enjoyed the festival." He was glad they hadn't been there because he could only imagine the questions they would be asking if they'd caught him working the muffin stand with Rosie. He had no hope, though, because he knew Brad would tell them eventually. But for now, maybe he could relax and not have to explain himself right from the start.

Though he'd just been helping out like a good neighbor, they might get ideas. And that was the last thing he needed right now.

He moved around the kitchen counter that was also an island in the big kitchen. His dad was already sitting on one of the barstools.

He clamped him on the back and rolled his eyes while grinning. "Forgive her—she can't help herself."

They all knew that Maryetta Sinclair had the heart of a mother hen and the tenacity of a bulldog. She loved her babies like newborns, despite them all being somewhere in the vicinity of the thirty mark.

"I know," he said, shooting his mom a smile when she looked up from slicing the tomatoes.

"I'm glad you enjoyed yourself. And your dad is right, I can't help myself," she said. "I've been worried that it was all a dream and that you might come over tonight and tell me you were leaving again. And, I have to say, it's been a comfort knowing you're so near. Now tell me, what have you been up to? We haven't seen you as much as I thought we would once you were back in town."

"I've been getting settled, Mom, and working on the cottage, and I started at the clinic too." He had missed seeing his parents, but couldn't let them think he'd moved home to spend every moment at their home.

She waved a hand. "I'm glad you're settling in and, really, I don't see your brothers all that much either. Just when I cook dinner and you all come over." There was a teasing lilt to her voice. "Dinner, my secret weapon."

"Always has been," he said, chuckling.

Growing up, they'd always joked that her boys were never going to leave home because she took too good care of them. But of course, they all left home and always came over once a week or every two weeks when she had dinner. At least, everybody who was in town did. This was only his second time coming over since arriving back in town. He felt guilty, but he didn't want her to start thinking that he was going to be living at her place and eating her food all the time. He had his own life and had been independent for too long.

Still, it was great to be back.

His dad picked up his coffee mug and paused midway to his lips. "I heard Doc say he was pleased with how you've been helping out at the clinic. What do you think about that—are you liking it?" He took a sip of coffee after asking the question, as if it wasn't something he just needed to know.

Adam knew differently. Adam knew that they had always hoped he would move back here and take over the practice. He hadn't wanted to be a small-town doctor. He'd had his sights set on something more challenging and now he was home, with no idea what he wanted out of the rest of his life.

His parents, though, knew exactly what they wanted. Grandchildren. But so far, none of their children had married and given them babies to fawn over.

He hoped they weren't counting on him to fulfill that need for them anytime in the near future. Not while he was in the midst of coming out of the tunnel he seemed trapped in. Maybe one of his brothers or sisters would suddenly fall in love and marry the partner of their dreams and have a baby soon. His parents were very nurturing and it was only natural they were eager to have grandkids to play with and love. But his brothers and sisters were all building careers, so he didn't see it happening anytime soon.

"I've enjoyed it, actually. Still, don't get your hopes up too much. I haven't promised to take that on full-time and I'm pretty sure that I'm probably not going to." He paused, then thought he needed to make it even more clear. "It's been good, but I'm not ready to commit to anything right now. I'm up for helping out and it's helping me by letting me see another way to practice medicine. But all I can say right now is that I'm not sure."

His thoughts went to the kid. The kid he'd lost on the operating table. The kid in his heart of hearts he knew he should have been able to save. But he hadn't been able to get the fragments out and the bleeding stopped in time... Questions ate at him. Mainly, if Adam hadn't been so burned out and tired, would he have worked faster and would the boy have lived? Had he missed something that could have saved Mikie?

Thinking he might have been so tired and burned out that he'd missed something ate Adam alive whenever he let his defenses down…usually late at night. He was able to cope during the day, staying busy, but at night it drove him from bed.

Not wanting to let his mood slip into deep waters while visiting his parents, he picked up a tortilla chip and dipped it into his mother's special cheese dip. "How have you been doing?"

His dad grabbed a chip and dipped it into the dip. "Great. You know we're getting older, though, and all of our children are too. So, we are figuring someone is going to get married soon."

"I'm not convinced," his mother said. "I'm starting to lose hope. I know, I know—you've got to get married before you have your babies, so if there are no girlfriends or boyfriends on the horizon, then babies aren't either. It's not like I'm sitting at home in a rocking chair just waiting to hold a baby, but…"

His dad looked at him and raised his eyebrow. "The day your mother sits down in the rocking chair, I'm going to start bringing her to the doctor. She's always been too active to sit and rock. She might need to sometimes—however, she doesn't, so when she does start I'll be suspicious that something is wrong."

His mom had always been active. A take-charge kind of woman who'd wrangled six kids with a lot of laughter. She would enjoy being a grandmother. But she could continue to count him out on being helpful on the subject. He was not ready.

Instead of saying so, he agreed with his dad. "I would be worried too. You still doing your yoga, Mom?"

She laid the knife down and scooped the tomatoes into the salad bowl. "Yes, I am. But if I want to get a rocking chair, I will." A mischievous glint sparked in her eyes. "*Speaking* of yoga," she drew the word out, "Lila Peabody was in my class this morning and she said that they had a really good time when you showed up at the new bakery and helped them prepare muffins for the festival, and *then* helped sell them the next day. I wasn't going to ask about it… okay, yes I was. But I was waiting for you to bring it up. But now that you've brought up yoga, I just can't help myself."

He should've known she would know. Gossip traveled fast in a small town, even a beach town like Sunset Bay.

"And back to the subject of grandchildren, I am beginning to think all of my children are conspiring together to never give me any."

"Now, Mom, don't get any ideas. I'm not dating and have no immediate plans in my future to do so anytime soon."

"But you are enjoying working at the clinic and Doc needed help so badly."

"Yes, he did, but I haven't committed to becoming his full-time relief or that settling here in town is what I will ultimately choose to do."

Adam had always been a planner. He'd never planned to marry until his life was settled. With his career taking all his time, he'd planned to put it off until his career was on the trajectory he was satisfied with. That hadn't been as easy as he'd thought because promotion and upward opportunity had come rapidly. He'd thought the sense of growing dissatisfaction was simply because he hadn't found the hospital trauma unit he felt at home in. Then disaster had struck and everything collapsed. And here he was, back home where he'd started, sitting in his parents' home and contemplating his future.

"Your mother just can't help it. She's been obsessed with this lately. I'm beginning to think she will hang out her matchmaking sign soon."

"It's not as if that's all I do." She laughed and added a stack of bowls beside the cheese dip. "But it is a thought."

It was time to change the subject. "I'm glad you're doing your yoga. It's good for you."

"Yes, it is. Lila says the new baker is lovely and that not only did you help them prepare for the festival, but that you spent all day at the festival helping her sell the muffins and other goodies to the crowd."

Rosie filled his mind, as she had every moment he let his guard down. Her smile and sunny disposition warmed him. His mother would love her. And now that she'd heard about her from Lila, it was more than likely that she would be heading over to the bakery to check Rosie out. And he knew there would be no stopping her. His mother was a very determined woman when she set her mind on something. He could not miss the spark of anticipation flaming in her sea-blue eyes. Eyes he inherited from her. She'd been holding back this excitement, he realized, but now that it was out, there would be no stopping her.

But he hadn't just inherited her eyes; he'd also inherited her determination. His dad, Leo, was more laid-back, content to watch his wife lead the way. Adam could have used a little of that easy contentment. But that hadn't been the ultimate plan. Now he steeled himself to go softly.

"Lila says this bakery owner is your neighbor, too. That she lives in the cottage beside you. Not Lila, but the young woman—Rosie, I believe her name is. Lila says she is lovely. I can't believe I haven't met her yet. But then, I haven't gone into the bakery yet. Though Erin said the muffins are to die for."

Lila was right about that. She was lovely. "Mom, yes, Rosie is my neighbor and yes, there is truth in the fact that she is lovely and she can bake muffins so good that once you've had one you won't be able to stop. I can't deny it. But don't get any ideas. Again, I am not looking for a wife. It is completely not the time in my life for that. You'll have to set your sights on one of your other children."

Brad walked in at that moment and Adam had never been so grateful in all of his life.

"Hey, what's Mom supposed to try out on one of us?" Brad was a big guy, tall at nearly six-four, and powerful. He grinned as he strode past Adam and wrapped his arms around his mother in one of his bear hugs. Then he gave her a big kiss on the cheek.

She laughed as he released her. "I'm glad you're here."

He leaned against the counter and immediately grabbed a chip. "My favorite mother has made my favorite dip. Now what devious plan do you have for one of your poor children? Do I need to prepare myself in case I'm the poor sucker you choose? Are you returning me to the hospital? I don't think children are returnable."

Adam stared at his brother, who, as always, was never at a loss for words. Brad was about as spontaneous as Adam was reserved and enjoyed getting a laugh out of those around him. It worked well in his line of work as the head of the fire department and a leader in the emergency response team for the National Disaster Response Team. He could put people at ease in just a few words. Where Adam did that in a quieter manner in the trauma unit, Brad did it with good-natured humor. It was a gift Adam both envied and, sometimes, growing up, had made him want to throttle his younger brother. Because once wound up, he could carry things way past welcome.

"Your mother is just putting out feelers for which of you is going to marry and give her a grandbaby to spoil. She thinks you've all gotten together to conspire against her getting any grandbabies."

At his dad's words, Adam hitched a brow at his brother, who let out a long whistle and held his chip-wielding hands up in a whoa-hold-on-a-minute signal.

"Do not set those pretty eyes on me, Mother dear. I'm not interested. I've been burned and, being a fireman like I am, I know when to stay out of the flames."

She looked sternly at him. "You are going to have to move forward, Brad. It's been two years. Goodness, it's not like you to just give up after disappointment. You've never been a quitter and I don't expect you to be where love is concerned."

"Give the pep talk to someone else." Brad put a well cheesed-up chip into his mouth and gave her a comical back-off look that Adam and his parents all understood was serious.

He'd had a really hard time after his childhood sweetheart suddenly broke off their relationship and married someone else. Adam knew his brother had felt heartbroken and devastated at the same time. He would have felt the same way. None of them understood what happened with the woman they'd all assumed would be their sister-in-law. Adam didn't blame Brad for his wariness to jump back into the dating game, much less a real romance and commitment.

And opening up his heart to love again was another issue altogether.

Their mother sighed. "You boys always did have minds of your own. I'm not losing hope, though."

"You still have four more kids to pick on. That's the reason you had so many of us, isn't it?" Brad said, more of a statement than a question. He laughed, showing that he was okay now that the conversation wasn't focused on finding his happily-ever-after love. "It really is, isn't it?"

That made his parents chuckle and shoot each other conspiratorial looks.

Leo nodded. "We did discuss that when we were having children."

When Brad and Adam looked at their mom, she put her hands on her hips. "Don't look at me like that. I haven't been hounding you boys. I've been very patient, I believe. But enough is enough. It's time for all of you to settle down."

Brad and Adam locked slightly alarmed gazes. There was no mistaking the determination in his mother's voice. She was more upset about this than either had assumed. It was clear she wanted grandchildren.

Brad hitched a brow, the one his mother could not see from her angle beside him. Adam couldn't do the same since Maryetta Sinclair had a clear view of him from the other side of the counter.

He sighed and then looked directly at his mother. "Mom, there is no reason to get all worked up over something you really don't have any control over. You want us all to marry the right person, I know this for a fact, so just let this ease along like it's supposed to."

"Is it safe to come in?" Their sister Erin peeked around the hallway doorframe. "I don't want to enter while the baby talk is going on. I'm not surrendering, so I am not waving a white flag. You got that, Mom?"

Adam laughed. Leave it to Erin to state it like it was. "What say you, Mom—is the baby talk over for the time being?"

His dad was grinning as his mother heaved a frustrated breath. "Oh, for heaven's sakes, Erin. Come in here and give me a hug. I never expected you to be the first to give me babies anyway. You are just too independent and only now getting settled with your bed-and-breakfast. So, you are off the hook."

Erin—all blonde, blue-eyed, five-foot-eight inches of her—bounced into the room, grinning. "Well, why didn't you say so? I'd have come in fifteen minutes ago instead of standing out there in the hall letting you have a go at these two misfits."

Erin draped her arms around him from the back and whispered, "Sorry, I just couldn't come in and save you."

He laughed again. "I'll get you back."

"Ha, not if I get you first." She let him go and moved to give their dad a hug, then scooted around the end of the counter to punch Brad in the ribs before giving their mom a hug.

Then she looked brightly at them all. "Now, what's for dinner? I don't think Tate is showing. Isn't he in Bali or somewhere? I honestly can't keep up with him. And Cassie is out of town too. Right? And Jonah will probably be late as usual, since there always seems to be one of his client's boats breaking down that he has to go tow back to the harbor. I tell you, owning a boat rental business in a busy tourist town is very inconvenient at times like this. I, however, am here and ready to relax. I've been buried in business at the B&B and everyone only emptied out this morning, since the festival is over and all. Now I'm ready to chill."

"You're right. It's just us," Leo said. "Jonah will show up if he can. So, let's get to it. I've been smelling that pot roast cooking all day and I don't think I can hold out much longer."

"Fine, I get the hint. Let's eat." Maryetta turned and crossed to the stove.

The moment she turned her back on them, they all mouthed a thank-you to their dad. He winked at them, then headed around the counter to help pull the roast from the oven.

"Whew, that was close," Brad whispered before he ate another chip.

"I heard that."

"Sorry, Mom." He rolled his eyes at them. "I meant, that smells fantastic. What can we do to help?"

She turned and smiled sweetly at them. "Fall in love with someone and start growing this family."

Thankfully, she laid off them for the rest of the evening, but by then it was too late for Adam because he had a cute baker on his mind who refused to go away. He was relieved Brad hadn't talked more about the festival and brought her up.

Jonah showed up right before they got up from the table.

"Sorry I'm late. Had an emergency. A boater lied about knowing how to drive a boat and got himself into a bind. I had to go out and rescue them."

Adam's brother loved his work. Owning his boat business allowed him to be on the water or near it every day. Jonah had never planned to live anywhere but Sunset Bay. Why he hadn't married yet was a mystery to him because he had been settled for the last few years and seemed like one of the town's most eligible bachelors. It hit Adam that he was so disconnected from his family that he should know more about their lives. It just showed how self-absorbed he'd been in his own career.

It left him with an unsettling feeling in the pit of his stomach. One more downfall to add to his list of regrets.

"You look tired," his mother pointed out. "Did you have another emergency last night that kept you up?"

He did look tired. Weary, in fact. "Yes, one of my customers returned our largest boat late and most of my cleanup crew had a mutual friend's wedding to attend, so that left me to work overtime cleaning it up and getting it ready to be picked up this morning by another client. When fishermen come to town to fish, they want their boats on time. It was a late night and an early morning."

"Why have all my children chosen careers with such stressful hours? It's no wonder I'm having trouble getting any of you to get married."

At Maryetta's words, Jonah shot them all a questioning look.

"Mama is a little stressed out about the subject of grandchildren," Erin warned.

Jonah grimaced. "Well, wow, I hate that I missed out on this dinner conversation. Matter of fact, I might have another emergency in the wings that I need to get back to." He laughed when he got a warning swat on the arm from their mother as she moved to get Jonah a glass of tea.

"I'm not going to run you off, since I could tell I almost ran off your brothers and sister. But, just so you are aware, I am ready for this family to grow. Don't you have any customers who are eligible or have daughters looking for a handsome, successful businessman who'd make an amazing husband and father?"

He rubbed the back of his neck. "I'd rather not have this conversation."

His mother glanced over at him from the open door of the refrigerator. "I do not know what I am going to do with all of you. And Adam, don't think I'm forgetting about this new neighbor of yours who owns the bakery. She sounds perfect and you need to pay attention."

His dad chuckled, and Adam and the rest of them just had to hope their mother didn't get any crazy notions to take up matchmaking. As it stood, after learning about Rosie, Adam realized he was now at the top of the list. And he was having a hard enough time trying to figure out the next phase of his life without that added complication.

Besides, he had his pretty neighbor on his mind enough; he didn't need anyone pointing her out to him. He knew exactly where to find her.

Erin sat up straighter and plopped her elbows on the table. "What? You met Rosie the baker? I was too busy with my guests to make it to the festival myself."

"He met her," Maryetta called.

"Yes, he did," Brad whispered, leaning in and winking at Erin.

Her mouth fell open and her blue eyes twinkled. "She's nice."

"How do you know her?" Adam asked Erin. Small towns were notorious; how could he have forgotten?

"I don't know her well. She hasn't been here long, but I bought a bunch of her muffins and pastries and some quiche for my guests recently. She is a delight, and so helpful."

"She's his neighbor," his mother added, setting tea in front of Jonah and smiling. "And I had already heard she was lovely, and now you say she's a delight. I'm thinking she sounds amazing. I'm going to get a muffin—"

"Mom." Adam narrowed his eyes at Erin, but she just smiled and continued to dig a hole for him.

"Your neighbor?" Erin said. "How perfect. You should ask her out. Really, Adam, you should."

Brad looked sympathetic but held his hands up, bowing out of the conversation.

Adam didn't hesitate. "You, my sister, need to worry about who you're going to date and not get caught up worrying about me."

"Or me," Brad added, obviously deciding he needed to reestablish his stance. "Just in case you get any ideas."

Jonah laughed, watching them, and took a bite of roast beef. "Same here. I don't need my mother *or* my sister meddling in my love life. I'm doing just fine."

Adam was glad to have his brothers on his side. And they managed to make it out of there soon after with promises from both mother and sister not to meddle.

But they'd stirred things up for him, and as he left his parents' home he had Rosie on his mind. Everything that had been said about her tonight was true. She was lovely, and delightful, and she was perfect marriage material as far as he could tell.

And she lived next door to him. He had a great opportunity to get to know her better.

But he wasn't ready to pursue anything serious right now. He was infatuated with her; that was all this was. He enjoyed her company. She was a good distraction from the dark emotions and questions he couldn't shake.

When he was around her, everything seemed better.

He just didn't need anyone getting any ideas. This wasn't good timing. His career was on hold and his life seemed to have stalled. He was a big picture guy. He'd known since he was in his teens that he wanted to be a trauma doctor and he'd worked hard to make that happen. He'd known what he wanted and where he was going. Now, for the first time in his life, he didn't know what he wanted, nor did he have a big picture plan. He'd come home to figure things out. To get some distance and gain perspective.

And then he planned to make the next step in his

life.

He hadn't planned on moving next door to Rosie. He hadn't even known someone like her existed.

She was just a walking ray of sunshine, and every time he was around her the gloom of his existence seemed less dark.

He felt pretty out of control where she was concerned. As if he were riding in a runaway rollercoaster and he had absolutely no control over where he was headed.

It had him pretty freaked out, now that he thought about it. What was he going to do?

CHAPTER NINE

Rosie was potting a geranium on Wednesday after the festival. The sun had gone down and she was doing it by the light of her porch. It had to be done, though, because the poor thing had been sitting there in its temporary pot since Saturday when she'd bought it as she was leaving the festival. The vendor had been closing up and as she and Adam had finished loading up their supplies to carry back to the bakery. She'd told him to wait, that she'd wanted to buy a flower. To her surprise, he'd followed her to the booth and insisted on buying the flower for her.

She had never had a man buy her flowers—not that these were to be misinterpreted as flowers in a romantic way; it was just a pot plant that she'd wanted. She should have insisted on buying it herself, but he'd already taken out his wallet and handed the money over to the man. If she'd insisted, it would have seemed rude and, well, to be honest, she liked that he'd bought her the plant.

But she'd been busy the last few days and hadn't had time to repot it, until tonight. It would be in bad form to let the poor thing wilt because it was root bound.

"You, my pretty, are going to brighten up the entrance to my home." She patted the dirt, smiled and took in her handiwork. The pot she'd placed it in was an old clay pot she'd rescued from a trash pile on the way home from work a few weeks before, and she'd set it at the back of the house, out of sight, until now. After a bright coat of white paint to match her shutters, it was like having a big smile greeting anyone who came to the door. The bright-white pot and the brilliant red flower contrasted well with her periwinkle blue house and yellow door. She was smiling as she stepped to the sand and studied it in the porch light. It went very well with her window boxes of flowers and completed the look she had been hoping for.

"Hey there, neighbor, imagine meeting you here at this hour."

She spun to find Adam standing between their houses. He looked good in his jeans and a white polo shirt that exposed his toned, tanned arms. His light-brown hair was getting lighter with every day he spent in the sun. In the light from the glow of her porch, it seemed almost sandy-blond now.

"Hi," she said, when she realized she'd been gawking at him. "Sorry, you startled me and I was lost in thought."

"I know. I was standing here for a couple of seconds before I said anything. What are you staring at?"

She smiled and waved him over. "This masterpiece. The one you helped with when you bought that pretty plant."

He came to stand beside her, close enough for her

to feel the warmth of his body and smell the light scent of his cologne. "Wow, that's really pretty. You have a knack for making everything pretty."

"Thanks." She crossed her arms and turned toward him. "So, how are you?" He looked so good. She'd thought of him a lot since the festival. Caught him sitting on his porch and longed to go out there and sit with him. But she hadn't. What had come over her? He'd been so helpful and she'd been thinking about his words that night he'd taken her home after baking muffins. He'd opened up to her. Told her that his work had been part of what was keeping him up at night. Putting those shadows in his eyes.

She was finding that she wanted to eliminate the shadows. She told herself it wasn't any different than the desire she felt to help everyone have a better day. Nothing different at all.

But deep in her heart, if she were honest with herself, she knew he was different.

"I've been good. I went to my parents' house for dinner with the family."

"Oh, I'm sure that was fun."

He looked comically wary. "You might not say that if you'd been there."

She laughed, just from his expression. "Well, you can't just throw that out there and then leave me hanging. What are you talking about?"

He shifted and jammed his hands in his pockets, then leaned back on his heels momentarily. "Let's just say that my mom has declared that she is tired of waiting on her children and told us it's time to get married. Not word for word but close."

Rosie caught the tension in his words. "That's intense. Did you all run from the room, screaming?"

He laughed but she sensed he was more stressed about it than he let on.

"No, but close," he admitted with a shrug of one shoulder. "It's a little bit sad for her, I guess. With six of us and not one of us married, I guess a mother longing for grandchildren has a right to get impatient. It is hard to believe none of us are even in a serious relationship at the moment. At least, not that I'm aware of. It was pretty intense." He chuckled.

Despite his chuckle, she got the feeling again that

he might not have been completely teasing. "You are stressed." She met his gaze and saw the flicker of surprise.

"Yeah, I think I could use a destressing walk on the beach. Would you want to take a walk with me?"

His question was so appealing on so many levels and yet she hesitated. Her thoughts told her this could be a major step in her future because she felt more for Adam than she could understand. *Was she ready to let her defenses down a bit?* She halted her thoughts. She was thinking too seriously.

Thinking too much when she needed to act.

"I would love to," she said, and his smile caused a flutter to spread through her like a thousand feathers falling from the sky. On fire.

"Good." His eyes lit up and he held his elbow out to her. "My day just got a whole lot better."

Hers too, she thought as he looked at her with deeply serious eyes that seemed to penetrate straight to her suddenly stumbling heart.

Yes, hers was better, she admitted, just from the moment she'd looked over and saw him standing there.

But she didn't tell him.

As they walked out onto the sand, her mind kept going to the moment when they'd been standing in her walk-in freezer and she'd thought he'd almost kissed her or wanted to. She'd woken up in the middle of the night a couple of times with that moment on her mind. It had left her feeling both giddy and disturbed. It was an odd combination that she just didn't know what to do about.

Moments later he'd told her to stop riding her bike and had caused her normally-hard-to-rile-up temper to flare. Then the man had spent the entire evening and the next day helping her. He'd been amazing.

Yes, the man confused her in all kinds of ways, with conflicting emotions battling it out inside her. But enough about herself; Adam needed to relax and she would help him do that. It was, after all, what she was good at.

"Don't you love the moment when the last light of day meets the dark waters on the horizon?" she asked, lightly gazing out toward the horizon that was already past the last of the brilliant sunset that had happened moments before he'd shown up. Now there was that faint glow just before the light extinguished and the stars began to spring out on the blackened sky.

"I hadn't really thought of that. I like the sunsets and sunrises and I like looking at the stars. But, I guess this moment..." He stared at the horizon as the light dropped away and darkness enveloped them. He looked at her and smiled. "This moment is good too, now that you point it out. Rosie, is there nothing you see that doesn't make you happy?"

She hesitated, as her eyes adjusted to the darkness. The moon would lift in a few minutes and there would be plenty of light. But even if she couldn't see him as well as she'd like, she could feel that penetrating gaze locked on her. She felt that strong pull to tell him her secret and she pushed it down. She hadn't planned to share that with anyone.

"I just look at every moment with fresh eyes. I try to enjoy each moment and that light disappearing like that is more of a signal that another day is done and I got to enjoy it. Midnight comes and goes each night, with no significant moment to announce that the day is done and a new day is officially starting. I guess my grateful clock goes by that light disappearing on the horizon."

His white smile widened in the moonlight. "Your grateful clock. I like that. Maybe I need to get one of those."

She laughed and squeezed his arm that she still had her arm linked with. "I think everyone needs one."

"Well, thanks for reminding me. Where did you get yours? I'll run right over tomorrow and pick one up."

She let the breeze calm her as she thought of all she'd been through to find her grateful clock. "Oh, I found mine at the end of a pretty rough day. Kind of like yours today." She was minimizing just how horrible a day it had been, but he didn't need to know that. This was about him, not her. "All you have to do is snap your fingers or close your eyes and say, *I will be grateful in all things*. Now, I must warn you that that is many times easier said than done."

He stopped their slow walk and she looked up to see that he had closed his eyes. *Dear goodness, even in shadow he was so handsome.* He opened his eyes and found hers with his.

"I now have my grateful clock. And thanks for the warning because I have a feeling my downward spiraling negativity is going to put up a really good fight."

She held his gaze. "You're a warrior now. You will succeed."

They stood there, staring through the soft light of the moon at each other, and Rosie knew that she was very grateful to be there with him.

"I've been thinking," he said. "About the bad experience you had surfing. Come surfing with me on Saturday. Can you get your helpers to cover for you?"

Surf. Panic clawed up her windpipe like a mad cat on a scratching post.

"Um, ah, I really don't think I want to do that."

"Come on. You are fearless. Let me help you get over that fear of the water and a surfboard. They go really well together but someone took you out too deep and too rough for your first lesson. These waters are perfect to learn in. All you have to do is trust me,

Rosie. I would never hurt you."

She hated this aspect of her life and the idea of overcoming it appealed to her. But the feeling of all that water clogging her air passages, pulling her down…it was just so powerful. And despite all her bravado about being a warrior on this subject, she let herself down every time.

Adam took her by the shoulders. His hands sent warmth and an overwhelming sense of security through her. And a need to feel those arms wrapped tightly around her. It was an all-powerful need that made her knees go weak and her lips to say the most unlikely things. "Oh, sure. If you promise—"

He cupped her chin with gentle fingers and tilted her face up so that he was looking at her with unwavering assurance. "I promise to keep you safe."

"Okay. Then let's do this."

His expression faltered and his gaze dropped to her lips and she suddenly thought he was going to kiss her like he'd almost done standing in the freezer.

"Right. That's exactly what we are going to do. Saturday." He smiled, then let go of her chin and took her hand. "Now, I think it's time to send you home and for me to get some sleep."

"Yes, good idea," she agreed. But as they headed back up toward the lights shining from their cottages, she wished with all her heart that he'd kissed her.

She was going to have to search really hard to find something about that not happening to be grateful about. Like she'd warned him, sometimes it was harder to do that than it looked.

CHAPTER TEN

On Saturday, Rosie followed Adam across the beach toward the blue waters of the ocean. She still couldn't believe she had agreed to let him try teaching her to surf. What had she been thinking?

That I am living life unafraid and looking for new experiences.

Right, that was her motto. But as the handsome doctor held her hand and led her toward the water, she wasn't so sure she wanted to embarrass herself in front of him. He'd said he wouldn't let anything happen to her and she did trust him. But she was a little clumsy.

She was pretty sure embarrassing herself was going to happen when she fell into the water and panicked. Panicking was not a pretty sight. She knew this but when he'd asked her again to let him teach her, she had agreed. Partly because she just wanted to spend time with him. And she wanted to overcome her fear. And it was better to try than to just surrender. That was not something she liked doing. And he had offered to help her win her battle.

The man knew how to be persuasive. She could still feel his fingers on her chin, the feel of his gaze on her lips. She wanted more. She wasn't going to pretend to herself that she wasn't interested. She just didn't know his level of interest. Today was all about exploring whatever this was between them.

And despite all of her misgivings, she followed him out into the water on this gorgeous, balmy day while wondering whether she should reconsider. The memory of the last time she'd attempted to surf was not going away. And as the waves slammed into her, panic rose in her throat. The memory of trying to find her way to the surface as she fought the choking spasms that had overtaken her that day several years ago got to her. She could feel the panic she'd had when she finally broke the surface and was immediately hit by another crashing wave. Now, she reminded herself that the surf had been harder off the coast of Hawaii than here. That today it looked as if she were going to have a hard time finding a wave to support a ride, much less get wiped out by one.

Still, the panic filled her chest and her heart fluttered sporadically. She tried to concentrate on the muscled shoulders of Adam. They were quite impressive and were recently tanned, with a tinge of burn because he'd been accumulating this new tan since arriving in Sunset Bay. As if sensing her thoughts, he turned toward her just as a wave splashed against his back and over his head.

He laughed, then studied her. "You don't have to look so terrified."

No telling what her expression had looked like, but obviously it had made him aware that there was turmoil brewing inside her. She'd warned him, not able to pretend all was right in her world.

"Are you okay?" He moved to her and took her arm with his free hand.

"I'm sure you can tell I'm a little nervous." The last part came out as a squeak as a wave splashed against her chest and lifted her feet from the sandy bottom and into deeper water. She clasped at her board and he steadied her while keeping his head above water as if he had floats on.

"You're going to be fine. Okay, climb onto the deck. Lay down, with your toes at the end of the board. Watch the line through the center of the board and align yourself with it straight through your body. When we get past the white waves, we'll be ready to practice coming up into the standing position like I showed you earlier. Remember—I'm right beside you." He let go of her arm as she managed to hoist her upper body on the board. They paddled out past the waves. Once there, he turned his board and she did, too, getting ready for the waves that would come soon.

"Remember, when the wave comes, feel it, then pop up to your standing position, feet shoulder width apart and on the center line, with knees slightly bent and arms out to help balance."

She nodded, feeling sick and wanting to hold on for dear life. But then she felt the wave and she knew she wasn't about to let herself chicken out. She would do this. Eventually.

She hoped.

He straddled his board, smiling, distractingly so. "You've got this."

She lost her fear in that moment, transfixed by the rivulets of water washing down his muscled body, and she blinked through wet lashes. *Focus, Rosie.*

Right. Focus and do this. She pushed up with her arms, then brought the first foot to the board beneath her. Happiness engulfed her as she managed to hop up and the second foot was beneath her on the board.

She was up! She was surfing!

It wasn't graceful, but for a brief instant, she stood on the board on a wave.

"Great job," he called.

She laughed, lost her balance and fell backward into the water.

Engulfed instantly, she sank deep, feeling the

sense of panic as she plunged beneath the waves. Then she felt his hands on her arms and she broke the surface.

"You had it."

"Ha, liar," she called and couldn't help the smile on her face, trying to feel positive and hoping the increasing panic would dissipate.

"Nope, I am not. If you get worried, let me know and we can go back to the shallow water and practice your moves."

They'd already practiced and she knew more practice wasn't what she needed. What she needed was to get out here and overcome the fear. If she could just get on the board once without taking a hard fall and a dousing by a hard wave, she might overcome the fear. She wanted to do this more than she could express. It would be a positive factor in this part of reaching her goal to overcome.

They paddled back out past an oncoming wave and waited for those that were farther out. She tried to relax as they waited for the wave that felt right.

"Now, this time be aggressive in your stance as the wave comes. Feel the flow and remember to have fun. If you go down, I'm right here. I'll get you."

She held his gaze, reassured that he would be there for her. This gave her a semblance of calm that helped somewhat. "Thanks, because the fear that I don't want to admit to is there. I guess it's the strength of the wave that rolled me over and held me down that won't get out of my mind. I'm going to defeat it, though."

"I have no doubt about that. These are not big waves—they're learning waves. Okay, this looks like a good one. Get ready. Here you go."

She'd seen it coming and was ready. His confidence in her gave her a warmth that she was glad to feel. As the wave came, she was in position. One minute, she was ready and pushed up so her feet were on the board. But the wave was stronger than the last and instantly she flipped forward into the ocean as the wave rocked her. She rolled beneath the surface, then felt strong arms wrap around her; in the next instant, she and Adam were above the surface. She coughed, but was thankful she hadn't taken on enough water to sink a ship.

"I've got you." Adam held her close as the waves continued to hit them.

She felt safe, aware of his arms wrapped securely around her. He kicked, pulling her backward with him as he let the waves carry them.

"Thanks."

"That's my girl. You did great. Ready to try again?"

She drew security from him and nodded. He'd proved that she wasn't alone out here and he would pull her out if needed. "I'm ready. Ready to see if I can at least stay on board longer than a nanosecond."

He laughed. "You'll get there. It's all about the feel of it and adjusting to it. Determination is a good attitude to have in this instance. Okay, grab your board."

She took hold of her board and he released her. She wished for his arms to be back around her as she took her board and headed back into the waves. If determination was a good friend to have right now, then she was good, because she had tons of determination. Determination was her middle name.

Adam watched for the third time as Rosie lifted up

onto the board and he braced for her to fall as she'd done the two times before. But she didn't, and his heart caught as her thin frame balanced and she let her knees loosen up to take the movement. She was riding the wave.

He wanted to cheer but was afraid she'd hear him and lose concentration, so he held his excitement inside and rooted for her like crazy in his own mind.

She backed up on the board and then moved forward, holding her balance as she stayed in the rhythm long enough for it to be a good confidence builder. Then she went down and he went after her. He'd enjoyed the feel of her in his arms earlier and was aware that she was thin, almost too thin. And he couldn't help but wonder if she'd been ill. The thought had crossed his mind before. Her legs had muscle tone, though small. His gaze had been drawn to them as she'd first climbed to the board and he'd watched them tremble before giving out and she'd tumbled into the crashing waves. She seemed like a newborn filly on legs that were unsteady as the blood flow tried to give them strength. On the second try, they were steadier and this last time they held. Still, as he watched her surf, he couldn't shake the feeling that she was also regaining her strength from more than the waves.

"Rosie, you did it," he said when they bobbed in the waves, looking at each other. She hadn't needed him to pull her from the water this time, but he wanted to. Wanted to use it as an excuse to hold her.

Her eyes sparkled as the blue topaz water rocked around her. "I did. I felt steadier. I think it'll be better next time."

"Maybe we need to rest before you take another run at it, though." He didn't want to risk her getting injured when her strength wore out.

"I think you're right." She turned and headed in and he went with her.

The beach was slow today. Not many people were here in the area in front of their bungalows that were semi-private, with the barrier of the tree line down from them and the stretch of wider sand farther up from them that was typical here on the sandy shores of Sunset Bay. These beaches weren't as wide as the shores of Windswept Bay or St. Petersburg but they were still beautiful. He had always preferred them growing up because they weren't quite as popular as the other beaches. They reminded him more of the less crowded beaches of Marathon Keys, another of his favorite places.

He had started to feel his head and maybe his heart healing as the days passed. Every day that he put between him and Chicago was a better day and he had to admit that part of that was due to Rosie. He could tell that given a few more attempts at surfing and she'd be just as graceful on the board as she was in the water.

He felt his gut pull as she strode from the water, clutching her surfboard and jogging through the water when they neared the shallows. She laughed when she reached the sand, dropped her board, then removed her ankle band. He did the same.

"I feel like I've had a load lifted from my shoulders."

He grinned at her. "And why is that?"

"Because I got to my feet and stayed up. Not long, but still I surfed. And I didn't get nearly drowned. That has been hanging over me for so long. I hate fear. I hate it with a passion and now, thanks to you, I've overcome this really frustrating irritation."

He placed his hands on his hips and studied her. "What makes you so unafraid? Other than this surfing fear you seem fearless to me."

She inhaled and reached for the towel she'd left beside her beach bag earlier. The sun warmed his back and dried the dampness from his shoulders as he watched her bury her face in the towel and then mop the rest of the water from her glistening body. He thought that she was using the moment to get her thoughts together. He knew instinctively that what she was about to share was important.

His pulse quickened when she lifted those gorgeous sky-blue eyes to his and there was hesitancy there. He waited, riveted to the expression on her face and those eyes.

She took a deep breath. "I was very ill. But Adam...I don't—" Her words broke off and she looked as if she wasn't going to finish what she'd started to reveal about herself.

Selfishly, he willed her to continue, wanting more

than anything to know what made Rosie the amazing Rosie that she was. "Go on," he said softly.

"I haven't told anyone in Sunset Bay about my past."

"You can trust me," he said, willing her to trust him. Wanting more than anything he'd wanted in a very long time for this beautiful, caring, sweet woman to trust him with her secrets.

"I nearly died."

The words were softly spoken but echoed between them like the bang of a hammer hitting a spike. He felt it like a blow. *She'd almost died.* "How?" He sank to the sand beside her. His knees felt weak.

"I need you to keep this fact to yourself. I'm not sure why I'm telling you. But…maybe it's because I feel like I can trust you. I've felt that way from almost the moment I met you."

He suddenly felt as if he'd just swam five miles upstream as their gazes locked and held and that undeniable attraction pulsed between them. She'd trusted him with a revelation that shocked him to his core.

He liked it very much and hoped equally as much that it was because she felt she could trust him as a man and not because he was a doctor. It hit him in that moment that he needed to be seen as someone other than a doctor in her eyes. He needed to be seen as a man.

He'd been living his life, striving to be a doctor for so long that he'd forgotten what it was to just be a man. A man that a woman would be attracted to and trust simply for the man he was—not the doctor he'd become.

It hit him in the reflection of her eyes that somewhere along the way he'd lost himself, the person, lost the empathy in the brisk, straightforward need to get things done and lives saved during the high-stress, high-stakes hours in the trauma units where there was no place for error.

CHAPTER ELEVEN

R osie inhaled sharply. *I told him my secret, that I'd nearly died.*

Told him the one thing she'd not wanted to tell anyone. Why had she done this? Now he would look at her with the pity that she'd wanted so desperately to leave behind. The look in his eyes had just shifted; she'd witnessed it.

Now, despite thinking it was best to keep her mouth silent, she'd opened her mouth and thrown herself under the bus by telling him.

His mesmerizing gaze held hers, reached into the

depths of her and she surprised herself again as the feeling welled up inside her to spill her *entire* story to him. What was wrong with her? Was it his being a doctor? Was it his bedside manner? What suddenly had her contemplating spilling all her secrets to him?

Or was it the fact that he was her neighbor…her new friend who'd helped her make and sell muffins because he'd known she was shorthanded and needed help? The friend who was now encouraging her to overcome her fear.

Her thoughts rolled, and she knew…it was as the man, not the doctor. The realization gave her a fizzy feeling in the pit of her stomach.

Given that she was a fan of doctors, because they'd been her angels in her fight to live through the cancer that had almost robbed her of her life, it really spoke well for him. As they stared at each other, she felt that undeniable pull between them tightening. She wanted to reach out and hug him. She wanted to kiss his cheek…oh goodness, who was she trying to kid— she wanted to kiss his mouth.

Wanted it in that moment, more than anything

she'd wanted since the day in the hospital that she'd realized how desperately she'd wanted to live.

He wanted desperately to kiss Rosie Olsen.

Wanted to wipe away her painful past and rewrite her history into a perfect fairy tale. The sun warmed their skin as they studied each other. The ocean breeze lifting flyaway strands of her blonde hair had him wanting to reach out and smooth it gently with his fingers. Instead, he reached for his T-shirt on the ground and then tugged it over his bare chest. He caught her blue gaze drift down, following the movement. Then he lost the connection as his head was lost in the nowhere land between the hem of his shirt and the neckline. As his head popped free of the neckline, he instantly caught her gaze shoot from his torso to his face and a blush tinged her pretty cheeks. He hoped he saw interest in her gaze that matched what he was feeling for her. And he suddenly wondered in a time like this how he could be thinking about his attraction to her.

"You can trust me. I'm so sorry you went through that. Are you okay now?" He had to know. She wiped her hair with the towel and avoided his eyes for a moment, and he wondered whether she was going to deny him any more of her history. Just when she had him hanging on the end of the hook like a bait fish.

"I'm fine. I had a really rare cancer with a very long name. The doctors and a new last-chance trial medicine pulled me back from death's door, and God too. It was two years of pain and uncertainty that ended well for me...not so well for many who I became close to on the trial. I'm forever grateful that it worked on me. But also, I harbor deep regret for those whom it didn't work for."

She blinked suddenly and he brushed a tear away that escaped from the corner of her right eye. "I'm sorry that it didn't work for everyone, but very glad that it worked for you. The whole thing had to be hard. But I've learned..." He thought of the boy; his heart clutched and a lump formed in his throat. He swallowed hard and forced himself to sound as normal as possible, though he heard the tightness in his voice.

"I've learned that life has a way of taking and giving, and not everyone gets the miracle. I'm glad you did."

She bit her upper lip and sniffed. "I'm grateful too, and something told me you would understand. You being a doctor makes it a little easier to talk about."

He tried hard not to let the disappointment of her words dig too deep. He was a doctor, but more than anything he wanted to be just a man to this beautiful, sweet woman. Now, more than ever.

"But," she continued, "I don't want anyone else to know because I, well, I don't want anyone's pity. But it's more than that. I don't want to have to relive it with others if they ask questions. I can't do it. I had to endure it from well-meaning friends for six months after I lived and something inside me just knotted up. I had plans and wants and I kept feeling like I was getting held down with pity and well wishes. It's a tangle of stuff in my head and heart that I felt terrible about but couldn't shake. In the end, I left and disappeared, only to turn up here where no one knew me. Where I could have a fresh start and do my thing. Bake and bring smiles to folks. I love brightening everyone else who is down or struggling or sick. I love being one of the people who gets to ease whatever they are going through with a token of goodwill by either giving them a muffin when I go to visit the hospital or the nursing home, or if they come into the shop to buy something from me. I love that."

He was smiling at her and she smiled back at him, looking a little embarrassed. He thought it was adorable. And he knew about all her muffin donations that she delivered with a smile.

And he got what she was saying. "Your secret is safe with me."

They were sitting close on the towels on the beach; he leaned back on one hand as his torso was turned toward her. She pulled her knees up and rested her chin on her knees, and turned her head so she looked at him with those big blue eyes.

"I know," she said. "You're a doctor, so I know you're trustworthy."

Again, it hit him that he wanted her to see him as a man, not a doctor. He leaned toward her, his fingers trailing along her jaw. "Rosie, you can trust me with your secrets because I'm a man who respects your need to start over. It has nothing to do with me being a doctor. I'm…" He wanted to say he was the man who wanted to kiss her. It was true, but he wasn't planning to say that. "Your friend."

A sweet smile spread over her heart-shaped face and she lifted her head. "Yes, you are."

Her gaze dropped to his lips and he found himself drawn in a little closer to her. She leaned toward him and then he kissed her. First, it was just the soft touch of his lips to hers, and then he shifted, bringing his hand up from where he'd been leaning on it, and he threaded his fingers through her unruly hair while he cupped her face with his other hand. And he continued to kiss her she melted into him. It was the most amazing feeling he'd ever felt. When she sighed and wrapped her arms around his neck, he wanted to pull her closer and let the kiss go on forever.

But thankfully he came to his senses and pulled back. Letting his forehead rest against hers, he tried to stop his world from spinning out of control. Rosie Olsen was completely flipping his world upside down.

"Wow," she whispered. "You really came through."

He laughed and pulled back to see her sparkling eyes and a slightly goofy smile. "Okay, so is that a good thing?"

She nodded. "I feel a bit like a schoolgirl. I'm twenty-five and never been kissed. Until now."

"What?"

Surely, he'd heard her wrong. He pulled back and stared at her. She was beautiful. But more than that, she was sweet and kind and adorable. There should have been fellas lined up from here to New York trying to give her kisses and roses and winning her heart. His stare caused her to blush.

"What's wrong with the men you've been hanging out with?" It was a stupid thing to say but the only thing that came to mind.

Her smile widened, then faltered. "I haven't hung out with any boys except you in a very, very long time. I wouldn't date while I was sick. I wasn't able to be in contact with anyone, had no future to speak of, and prior to that I was a little different than I am now. I was more reserved. Shy in many ways."

He was still trying to process the fact that she'd never been kissed, and the extent of her illness, and now, that she had been *shy* prior to her illness. And what did it say about him that she'd just told him she'd nearly died and all he could think about was kissing her the first time and now kissing her again?

"You look stunned," she said before he could figure out what to say. "I've been told your personality can change after a life-changing experience. For me, it was a decision. I had faced death and nothing could be scarier than that. It taught me life was short and that I should go after what I want."

"And that's why you opened your bakery?"

"Yes. I left my past behind and I came here and started over. But enough about me. You know that story, and now I'm rested, so…" She stood. "I'm ready to try that again."

He stood. "Your wish is my command. Lead the way."

She smiled and then ran toward the water. He watched her go, overwhelmed by her. She'd come so far and she was fearless.

With a lightness squeezing his chest, Adam grabbed his board and followed Rosie back into the water.

CHAPTER TWELVE

Lulu stood in the dog park across from the fire house biting her lip as she held three leashes in her hand. The dogs loved coming here to the fenced dog park and running free for a few minutes each day. It was part of her dog walking routine and…well, it gave her a few minutes each day to watch him. Fire Chief Brad Sinclair was gorgeous. She hadn't told Rosie that she had been harboring a huge crush on Adam Sinclair's brother for a very long time. It was her secret. No one knew.

It was a secret fantasy that she wouldn't tell

anyone. It was too embarrassing. Like at the festival she'd almost made a fool of herself. She always tried to avoid him and she'd been going to see Rosie when she'd almost walked out in front of him. She nearly killed herself ducking behind the Korney Korn trailer. She could only hope no one had witnessed her weird behavior. Even now, thinking about it made her pulse race. She couldn't bring herself to face him. And yet, she had this disturbing need to get glimpses of him.

She'd been coming to this dog park for two years, ever since she'd moved to Sunset Bay and spotted him working a fire in her neighborhood. The man had taken her breath away and she'd been hooked ever since…with the state of mind she'd been in when she'd moved here, her behavior was confusing.

The man was way, way out of her league. Hadn't she learned her lesson?

No. She'd even toyed with the idea of trying to meet him but then the great shrimp fiasco had happened. She cringed even now thinking about it.

She'd been eating alone one balmy summer afternoon at one of the seaside cafes when the waitress led him to a table across from her. She'd lost her mind the moment she'd locked gazes with him and he'd smiled at her. She'd been so nervous that she'd accidently hit her fork and sent the shrimp and red sauce flying straight into the center of her chest. She'd watched in horror as the red sauce splattered everywhere and the shrimp slid down her boob, leaving a trail of the red sauce all over her white tank top.

She'd been mortified, more so when she looked up to see horror on Brad's face. He'd reached across the aisle and handed her a napkin just as a tall, voluptuous redhead, who he must have been meeting for lunch, showed up and threw herself into his arms. Lulu hadn't waited around, she'd used the distraction as an escape. She'd grabbed her purse and headed to the restroom where she'd attempted to clean up the disaster. But the red stain just spread and it was horrible.

She'd practically hidden behind a fern until she could grab her waitress and pay, and had gotten out of there without going back to her table. Since then she'd come to the dog park always wearing dark shades and her hair pulled back in a ponytail. She stayed far enough away that he couldn't see her face, especially since she stood behind a large bush and watched him from afar. Like today. It was ridiculous and wrong on so many levels but she couldn't help herself.

Many days she didn't spot him at all and some days she glimpsed him. And then some days, like today, she got to see him as he talked with the other firemen or helped wash the large fire trucks. The man was just too handsome. Big and tall and nice. She always remembered he'd handed her that napkin. But then the redhead had shown up...Lulu was a redhead too but she was short and small, and hippy. She was not the kind of woman he dated.

She pushed her shades higher on the bridge of her nose and watched as he laughed at something the other fireman said, and her throat went dry. He had such a nice laugh.

Ever since the great shrimp fiasco, as she called it, she'd avoided him at all costs. If she saw him coming down the street, she went the other way. If she went to a restaurant and spotted him, she left or asked to be put in a different section. It was sometimes awkward, but so far she'd managed to avoid him.

But he was seriously getting in the way of her moving forward. Of her having a serious relationship with anyone. Because she found fault in every guy she dated. Not that she'd picked any winners lately...she hadn't picked a winner ever. Her ex-fiancé had proven that.

She was starting to panic. She wanted a family. Wanted a husband and kids. But Brad Sinclair had her stuck in a time warp. She had to get him out of her system.

And as if a sign from heaven above showing her the truth, a red sports car pulled into the firehouse drive and a dazzling black-haired beauty unfolded her long, long legs and got out of the Corvette. By that time, Brad had walked over to her and she'd immediately thrown her arms around his neck and planted an exuberant kiss on his lips.

Yep, Lulu needed to move on. Needed to let this obsession go.

She needed to face the truth—Brad Sinclair might

be her dream man, but she most definitely was not his dream woman. What truth was this anyway? She didn't understand why she acted this way. It was completely out of character for her. Did it have something to do with the event that shall not be mentioned? After what Tyson had done...she wiped a hand across her eyes, not wanting to think about him. How could she come here and immediately get this obsession with Brad after Tyson's betrayal? And after losing Justin...she pushed thoughts of her brother out of her mind. She couldn't think about Justin. Even after two years it was still hard to accept that he was gone. Her heart hardened against Tyson even more every time she thought about Justin. He had been one of the good guys. Tyson obviously hadn't been. Justin had been helping her cope with what Tyson had done. And then he'd been gone. Dead too young.

Her heart hurt...she knew she had to face the truth, face the fact that he was gone, but it was just easier not thinking about it.

Dogs barking drew her attention; it was time to gather the pooches and head out. There was no need to torture herself any longer. No need to look back at the past. She'd come to Sunset Bay to put distance between her and the onslaught of pain she'd left behind. She'd figure out this thing with Brad. Figure out why her focus had shifted to him the moment she'd first laid eyes on him mere days after moving to town.

With one last glance toward the firehouse where Brad and the bombshell were now talking, she walked away.

Maybe she needed to see a counselor or something.

Nope, she just needed a date. Needed to get the past in the past. Needed to start over. That was the entire reason she'd relocated here to Sunset Bay.

Her landlord had been trying for months to set her up with a friend's son. So be it, why not.

She'd never had a chance with Brad Sinclair anyway since she was always avoiding him. Now, she just needed to stop stalking him. Well, that description was a little harsh. Really, she had to walk the dogs, so she had as much right to be at the dog park as he had to be at the firehouse.

A date. A date would help. *Dates* would help. And she'd start with Mrs. Thompson's friend's son.

The week after she'd shared her first kiss with Adam had been a wonderful one. She'd felt relief at having shared her past with him, at having someone know even though she didn't want everyone to know. It felt right sharing the most intimate parts of her life with him.

"I tell you, Rosie, I'm beginning to think this lie that a woman with a dog can find a husband is a myth," Lulu said.

Her words pulled Rosie from her thoughts. She'd been distracted like that all week. Lulu stood on the other side of the counter, getting her morning coffee before picking up her first doggy clients of the day. She looked dejected and Rosie felt guilty for having let her mind wander to Adam instead of giving Lulu her full attention.

"I mean, don't get me wrong, I've met guys out there and gone on a few dates, but they were all bad.

The guys either couldn't stop talking about their exes or their jobs or sports. I don't know—I'm beginning to wonder if there is something wrong with me."

Was that despair she saw in Lulu's eyes? Alarm swept through Rosie. "Whoa. Wait. There is nothing wrong with you, Lulu. I'm confused. A few days ago you said you were done with men." Rosie took the muffin and the coffee she was about to hand over the counter and instead carried it around the end of the counter and nodded to a table. "You and me need to sit down."

Her friend followed her over to the table. It was early as usual when Lulu came in, so the place was empty. "You eat this and let's discuss your situation."

They took seats.

Lulu sighed. "I know I said that. But I didn't mean it. I had just gone on another disaster of a date so I swore off men for good. And then—oh Rosie, I just don't get it. Aren't there any good guys out there anymore? I mean...well, I keep holding out hope that there is, but I don't stand a chance...I mean, I really am about to decide it's better to just stop and get off this merry-go-round to nowhere and learn to love my life without a guy in it."

Rosie's thoughts shifted instantly to Adam. She had it bad. After spilling her secrets to him and feeling his arms around her and just spending time with him, she knew she was falling for him—and falling hard and fast. She kept trying to tell herself she needed to pull back, to lock her heart away again, that she was treading in dangerous waters where her tender heart was concerned, but she was struggling to keep a clear head where he was concerned.

They'd spent time together over the last week and shared several moonlight kisses, and despite having known him only a short while she was falling for him. She couldn't deny it. But something held him back and she knew it. She could tell that he hadn't shared with her like she'd shared with him.

Something kept him up at night and she still didn't know what it was.

"Lulu, I know this can be stressful—dating, I mean. But, if you lock up your heart and don't try, you might miss out on the gem among the rocks. The right guy is out there somewhere, and he'll come along at the right time."

Not looking convinced, Lulu bit into her apple-cinnamon crunch muffin and moaned. "Well, if I could just eat these all day long, it might be okay. This is fabulous."

Rosie smiled as much from the compliment as from the fact that her friend was suddenly trying to change the subject. "Good, but that's not the point. A muffin is not going to replace love."

"Why not? I love this muffin." Lulu's expression was defiant as she took another bite, more like a chunk, into her mouth and chewed.

"Well, that muffin doesn't have strong arms to hold you. Or...or lips to kiss you—" Rosie's thoughts went wayward again, thinking of Adam. Her heart squeezed tight. She cleared her throat and her mind right along with it. *This was about Lulu.* "I'm just saying, no need to rush or go out with anyone who doesn't just blow you away when you meet him, but don't just slam the door on possibility. Keep your heart open and then let it happen naturally. Who knows, the right guy might be just around the corner."

Or living right next door.

Lulu sighed. "Don't I wish. You might be right. I guess it's true you have to kiss a lot of frogs before you meet your prince. I just went on the worst date ever last night. My landlord has fixed me up three times this week and every time it was not good. One guy was so handsy that I had to threaten to tell my landlord how terrible he acted and that she would tell his mother. The wimp dropped me off at the corner and I walked home."

"That's horrible." Rosie was shocked.

"Don't worry. The next guy I say yes to better knock my socks off or it's a no-go. And then the mace is going with me, and if he gets handsy he gets squirted right in the eyes."

"Oh, well, that's more like it. You sound more like yourself now. I'm relieved you have a plan. And, Lulu, I'm always here if you need to talk." She remembered spotting Lulu at the festival. "Oh, I've been meaning to ask, what were you doing the day of the festival? I saw you run behind the Korney Korn truck and then peek out. I wasn't sure what you were looking at, but it looked like you were hiding from someone."

Lulu paled and looked suddenly...guilty. But why?

"I was hiding from a guy. I didn't want to run into him again, you know."

"That bad, huh?"

"Um, yes. That bad."

Lulu stood and Rosie did, too, as Lulu hugged her. "Thanks. You said just what I needed. I better go pick up Spaz and Sussi-Q, the terriers from he—well, you get the idea. I'm going to straighten out their attitudes today. Just like you did mine. Thanks for everything." She picked up her half-eaten muffin and her paper cup of coffee and headed out.

Rosie watched her go, feeling relieved and a little stressed. It was one thing to give advice and a whole other thing to take it. Could she take her own advice?

The door opened just as she went back around the counter. Gigi was scheduled to come in at seven-thirty, just before the really busy time started, but it was only seven. Instead of her helper she was really glad to see one of her new regular clients enter the shop. Erin was in the middle of getting a bed-and-breakfast going. She'd recently opened enough to begin taking bookings. And that meant orders for Rosie. They'd never really talked much, other than when Erin had come in to make the order and then pick them up. Rosie hadn't gotten her last name, and even if she had she was really bad about remembering people's last names. She was a first-name kind of gal, but if she was going to start doing more business with Erin, maybe she needed to keep better records. She would get her name today.

"Erin, how are you?"

"Good morning, Rosie." The pretty blonde smiled a brilliant smile that reminded Rosie of someone but she couldn't put a finger on it. "I have to compliment you that your muffins and Danish were a hit with my guests over the festival weekend. And the quiche disappeared instantly. I have some more bookings for this weekend and would love a repeat order."

"That is wonderful to hear. I'm so glad your guests were satisfied. I hope the B&B is going great."

Erin nodded, a twinkle in her eyes. "It's going very well. How about the bakery—is it doing as good as it appears?"

Rosie didn't really discuss her business with anyone—actually, no one ever asked in the short time that she'd been opened, but just assumed that it was doing well. She had a lot of traffic here on the corner of Seashell and Main. "It does well. But I am always very glad to have new steady customer orders, like yours, to help me along."

"And I'm glad I'm starting to get business so I can give you those orders. I hear you had a great day at the festival. I *hear* you had a very handsome helper too."

Rosie paused. This was just what Birdie and the girls had said, that the women were going to start chasing after the handsome new doctor in town. And of course, because Adam had been helping her that day, naturally they'd come here asking questions. A murky sense of jealousy drifted over her mood and she had to force a smile. She would not let negativity overtake her. She would not.

"Yes, that was Doctor Adam Sinclair. He was

really great to help me out in a pinch when my helper got sick and couldn't back me up that day. He's a great guy." There, she'd said the truth and tried not to think about Adam having someone as beautiful as Erin interested in him. Of course, with as gorgeous as he was and as nice and perfect, the man would have all kinds of women interested. It was a wonder she didn't have a mass of women in here asking about him.

Erin's eyes danced, and why not? Rosie had just given her everything she needed to know about Adam and now she was free to look him up.

"I'm so glad you liked him," Erin said, startling Rosie. "And he's always been that kind of guy. Always willing to step in and help me anytime I asked. That is, until he moved away and his career took over. It's really great to have him home. And I can't tell you how happy I am to know you've been spending some time with him."

Confused, Rosie paused, pulling the muffin box from the stack under the counter. She'd reached for it as a distraction. She straightened. "You know him? I mean, it sounds like you know him well."

"I do." Erin grinned. "And I'm sorry I didn't explain. I guess I was being a little too mischievous. Adam is my brother. I'm Erin *Sinclair*. I don't think I've ever told you my last name. If I did, it was the first time I came in here and you've probably forgotten that."

Relief so profound it was scary slammed into Rosie. *His sister. This beautiful woman was his sister, not competition.* This was the blonde she'd seen that day from her window. The knowledge was even more profound. Was Rosie in it to win Adam's heart? The knowledge that she'd looked at Erin as competition said more than she'd admitted to herself. "His sister." The relief sounded in her words and Erin's smile widened.

"That's me. And to be honest, I don't need the muffins until Thursday evening so I'll come by then. I just couldn't wait that long to come by and see if you enjoyed my brother's company like I'm hoping you did. And he's your neighbor, too, I understand. That's very hopeful."

Hopeful? Rosie felt a bit conflicted admitting

something like that to Adam's sister, but she couldn't lie. "Yes, he's amazing. And yes, he's my neighbor."

"Great. Don't worry. I'm not here to get into your personal business, but I will tell you that I want my brother to move back here permanently. And I am hopeful that maybe if he finds the right woman that will happen."

"He's not staying here permanently?"

"Well, we don't know for certain. All he ever wanted growing up was to be a trauma doctor. Couldn't head off fast enough to busier places to work. But now, he's back and working on a fixer-upper to flip while he works out whatever it is that has him pausing his career. I'm not sure if he'll leave. But the fact that I'm hearing he's spent some quality time with you is fantastic. Anyway, I'm really not a nosey person but wanted to come by and let you know that he's my brother, and I think this thing between you two is wonderful. Oh, and don't be surprised if my mom drops by to check you out. She's as thrilled as I am to hear Adam is seeing someone. Maybe you and I could have lunch sometime. I'd love to get to know you better. And my sister Cassie would enjoy it too."

Shock and trepidation swamped her. "That sounds fun." She hoped Adam wouldn't have a problem with her getting to know his sisters. She really wanted to start making deeper connections with women her age. But Adam's sister, was that the right person? She started to clarify to Erin that she and Adam weren't actually dating or anything but the door opened and the morning crowd started filing in.

"Wonderful," Erin said, waving two fingers at her in goodbye and heading for the door. "See you later. I'll be by on Thursday for the order."

And then she was gone.

And Rosie needed a very, *very* strong cup of espresso.

On Thursday, Adam worked the clinic. It was a busy day, with all manner of illness going around. By the time he left, washing his hands for about the hundredth time before leaving the building, he was ready for fresh air and a run down the beach. He still hadn't gotten used to the slower pace of the doctor's office, but he was realizing that he got a lot of satisfaction out of seeing patients and helping them. He was tempted to stop by Bake My Day but didn't. He'd been going by there almost every day since Saturday's surf lesson and he needed to pull back a little and try to get some perspective on what he was feeling for his neighbor. Being around Rosie made him forget every dark emotion that had driven him from his career. And instead of making him feel better, it was making him feel worse.

He felt guilt and deep regret about what had happened in that emergency room that night and he had no business forgetting even for a moment that he didn't deserve to forget.

Once home, he changed into his running shorts and left the house, glancing across the sand at Rosie's cottage. Her bike was home, which was odd at this time of day midweek. But he'd only given Rosie surfing lessons; he wasn't keeping tabs on her. Despite his curiosity, he continued toward the beach, breaking into a jog once he made it to the hard-packed wet area with the water gently rolling in and dampening the path ahead of him.

The beach was busier today, with school having let out and some of the rentals on the end of the beach starting to fill up. There were kids playing in the sand and the water's edge, with mothers and fathers watching closely or playing with them. Despite the knot that seemed to always be deep in his chest, he felt a contentment as he jogged. Coming home had been the right thing to do and yet there was unrest inside him.

Forty-five minutes later, he jogged back to his cottage and stopped short when he saw Rosie coming out of her cottage wearing a red dress and heels that set her legs off, making them seem endless, while the red dress showed her slight curves and made her honey blonde hair sparkle. She took his breath away, and seeing her, the knot that hadn't been helped by his jog seemed to ease—as it always did when she was near.

"Hi," he said, feeling an overwhelming longing to walk straight up to her, pull her into his arms, and kiss her. They'd taken a few more walks on the beach and shared a couple more kisses and he'd been in a real mess since the kissing had started. He'd craved wanting to feel her in his arms again and feel her lips against his, but the internal struggle wrestling inside him was strong. There was the feeling of excitement at the prospect of a developing relationship with her and there was also a soul-wrenching feeling that he no longer deserved to feel that flame of joy he felt when he was near her.

But despite the ongoing struggle inside him, one look at her and the joy was there. And when she smiled, it seemed to make the sun shine brighter.

"You look amazing." He just stared at her. She smiled and it hit him then that she looked as if she were going on a date.

Her smile widened and she ran a hand down the skirt of the dress in an almost nervous manner. "Thanks. I haven't dressed up in a very long time. Not in a dress, anyway. I feel a little awkward, to be honest."

"Don't. You're perfect." The words came out in a rush, and considering it was the truth, he didn't even think about pulling them back. Her cheeks tinged pink. "Who's the lucky guy?" So maybe those words he should have pulled back.

She looked startled. "Oh, no guy. Well, I mean, not like that. There will be some guys there, though. I'm helping with a very special wedding today at the retirement home. Red for true love is the theme."

Red was her color. "At the retirement home?"

"Yes, a dear, sweet couple of the ripe old ages of seventy-nine and eighty-two are tying the knot today and they requested a wedding cake made from my muffins. You should see it. It's the cutest, largest heart-shaped strawberries-and-cream muffin, or any muffin, that I've ever made."

"That sounds like fun. Do you do weddings often?"

"No, not really. Not like this. I don't do wedding cakes, being mostly a coffee shop type bakery. Cake decorating is just not my calling. But I do cupcakes, they're easy. But my muffins are the big hit and, well, I take muffins to the retirement home every other week and host the weekly social gathering. Clarence and

Belva bonded over my muffins and coffee. Helping them get together is one of my most cherished accomplishments."

He loved the way her face lit up talking about the older couple. "So is matchmaking another of your super powers?"

"No, hardly. I just happened to help with this. Would you like to come to the celebration? It starts in an hour. I'm going early to make sure everything is ready. But it should be sweet. And there may be dancing, and I can tell you the ladies at the home would *love* to have another handsome man to dance with."

The thought of dancing with Rosie was enticing enough to have him wanting to say yes. "I was planning on painting the front shutters this evening." It was true, but it held no appeal to him suddenly.

He saw a flash of what he thought was disappointment in her eyes.

"I understand. If you change your mind, it's at Sandy Shores Retirement Home. I'd better go. I see my ride pulling up."

A sporty little MINI Cooper swung into the drive and Mami waved, sticking her head out the open window. "Hello, Doctor Cutie-patootie."

He waved and laughed as he walked beside Rosie to greet the mischievous Mami. "You two look like trouble if ever I saw it."

"Don't you know it," Mami said and winked. "I only hope our Rosie here doesn't give anyone at Sandy Shores a heart attack in that pretty red dress. Doesn't she look divine?"

Mami was looking up at him with eyes that seemed to see into his mind and read his thoughts. "Yes, Mami, I have to agree."

He watched Rosie disappear into the passenger side. He had to lean down slightly and looked past Mami to see Rosie in the matchbox of a car.

Mami patted his cheek. "I think it might be prudent to have a doctor on the premises, just in case. Maybe you should climb in and join us." She batted bogus innocent eyes at him.

He tugged at his sweaty shirt. "I don't think you would appreciate that too much since I'm all sweaty after my run."

"Oh, I don't mind sweat. And I *hate* that I missed seeing you jogging. You need to alter your route so you're over on my side of town."

He laughed. "I like it just fine over here."

"Well, maybe I need to alter *my* route." She winked at him again. "Anyhoo, we need to run. If you change your mind, you should join us. I, for one, will save a dance for you just in case. And Rosie will, too—won't you, Rosie?"

"Sure. I did invite him but he has things to do around the cottage."

Rosie appeared to blush, though it was hard to tell because he couldn't see her as well as he'd like. He was tempted to crash the wedding but knew that might not be a good idea. And there were several reasons for that. One, he didn't deserve to feel what he felt when he looked at her and two, he might not end up settling here…and that wouldn't be fair to lead Rosie on.

He watched them moments later as Mami backed the matchbox out onto the street and then they shot off down the road like a bottle rocket with a short fuse.

193

Rosie really needed to get a car and not have to rely on the questionable driving skills of Mami.

Maybe you should go to the dance and give her a ride home. For safety's sake. The voice in his head had a very good point. He'd seen too close and personal the dangers of reckless driving and, not that Mami did a terrible job driving, she did seem like a distracted driver. She had been chattering away, looking at Rosie at the same time she'd put the car in gear and shot forward. If a car had been coming, it might have been disastrous.

He forced himself to walk back to the cottage and start getting the tools to remove the last of the shutters. The paint wasn't peeling as badly on the front face of the house as it had been on the beach side where the constant ocean wind wore it down. So, the rush to repaint wasn't a top priority. The rumble of a motorcycle had him turning in time to see Tate turn his Harley into his driveway.

Great, just in time, because Adam needed more of a distraction than scraping and painting to keep Rosie and the little red dress, and dancing, off his mind.

CHAPTER THIRTEEN

"You're back."

"Got back late last night. I fly out again in two days for a month, though. I'm doing some stunts for a movie."

Adam could have never imagined the life Tate lived. On the one hand, most guys envied him, with his never-ending array of adventures that came from his aptitude for seeking it out, and then jobs like this that he took when he got the call. But his brother lived out of a suitcase and that never appealed to Adam. It fit Tate, though. He'd always been the restless one.

"I'd ask if it's dangerous, but then you'd have to

tell me the truth and I'm not sure I want to know."

Tate gave a cocky grin that was well supported by the skill that he had to back up his endless desire to push boundaries. Adam understood that sometimes all the skill in the world couldn't save a life when their number was up. This should have reassured him on all levels of his life and it was the words Tate used once when Adam had asked him why he put himself at risk. Tate believed when his number was up, it didn't matter whether he was jumping off a cliff or stepping off a sidewalk. So why not live while he had the chance?

"Not so much. I'm just a stunt double for an A-lister. Should be interesting. I came by to see how you're doing since last time we talked on the beach. You were pretty down."

He had been, but he realized that that was before he'd met Rosie. There was no denying that he didn't feel as hollow inside as he had that day on the beach when he and Tate had talked. Tate had been the one to mention Bake My Day.

"I'm adjusting and I like working a few days at the clinic. I also took your advice and went by the bakery. You were right. It's hard to get out of there without a dozen muffins."

Tate grinned. "The baker is pretty, too. Don't you think?"

"Can't deny that." *What was Tate up to? Had he sent him there for the muffins or to meet Rosie?*

"Is that all? I thought for sure she would smile at you and that cloud of gloom would dissipate instantly. From what I could tell when I was in there, she's the real deal—a true ray of sunshine."

The exact words Adam always used for Rosie. "You're right about that, but what makes you think— were you trying to fix me up?"

Tate laughed. "Maybe. I just saw her in action, spreading sunshine around, and you were looking like you could use some."

Adam studied his brother, contemplating his situation. "Did you know she was my neighbor?"

"I did overhear her telling someone she lived in one of these cottages."

Adam lifted a single finger and pointed toward Rosie's home.

"She lives beside you? Aw, man, that's perfect." Tate didn't even try to hide how much that pleased him. "She's single, right?"

"Yes, she is. And she is very nice. She's a very special person."

Tate remained on his Harley but crossed his arms and stared hard at him. "And you like her," he said, slowly. "Well, I'll be. I have to say, I never fixed anyone up before. That's pretty dang cool."

"I didn't say we were dating. I'm not ready for that and I don't know that she is either."

"Look, Adam. I know that something happened that caused you to walk away from a profession you love and are very good at. I know that you're picking up the pieces. But you need to move on. You're a doctor. A highly skilled, highly regarded doctor. I did some checking and I figure it had something to do with that boy that I read about in the newspaper. It was terrible and so very sad. I saw you were the one who operated on him and I saw that his injuries were too massive to save him. Are you blaming yourself for that?"

Leave it to Tate to dig into his past. He found it oddly a relief for someone to know, and in that instant he came clean. "Yes, I do. I keep questioning if I missed something. I couldn't stop the bleeding. I can't help but wonder if I might have not come through for the poor kid. If he might still be alive if I'd not been the one working that night. I was tired, not feeling like myself for a while, maybe depressed some. I'm not sure my state of mind was right."

Tate hung his head for a moment. "You worked with what you had at the time, and it appears from what I read that *time* was what you didn't have. It wasn't your fault that poor boy got shot. Or that by the time he reached you there wasn't enough time to save him. I can't even imagine how hard that must be." His gaze drilled into Adam. "But what I can tell you with certainty is that I know you, and I know that you gave him *everything* you had to give in the amount of time you had to try to make a miracle happen. You need to let it go. Or learn to live with it. You're grieving for him, I think, and that just shows how human you are. But you're a doctor, brother. You can't let your grief take over your life. You have to pick up the pieces and move forward and help someone else."

Goosebumps prickled across Adam's skin and he let out a breath of frustration as Tate's words sank in.

He hadn't had time. But he'd held himself responsible because he'd been fighting the demons of burnout.

He knew his brother was right. Hearing the words of reassurance from Tate, who wouldn't say anything that he didn't truly believe, Adam let the truth sink in. He wasn't sure how Tate was so perceptive on this subject but maybe that was what he needed—an objective eye looking in. And time. Time to find his way.

His chest hurt and he blinked hard against the burn of tears. "Thanks. I needed that."

"You're one of the good guys, Adam. The fact that you don't have a God complex makes you even better at your job. Don't let what happened keep you from moving on."

"I won't."

"Okay then, my work here is done. Got to go. I'll see you when I get home."

A few minutes later, when Tate rode off down the street, Adam felt a weight lifted and found himself looking at his watch. He looked at the unpainted shutters, and then turned and strode into the house.

He was going to a wedding.

CHAPTER FOURTEEN

Rosie had made sure that everything was perfect for this special day. She felt jittery and keyed up and she knew it was from her meeting with Adam. While she set the reception table up and made sure the muffin cake was positioned perfectly, her thoughts were on her neighbor.

She'd had turned their day of surfing over and over in her mind. She had loved every moment she'd spent with him. And when he'd held her in his arms there in the water, she'd felt more alive than she'd ever felt. And then she'd sat right there on the sand and spilled her guts to him. But it had felt right. And she'd trusted him. She'd trusted him as a man, a friend. Not, as he'd said, just because he was a doctor.

Her world had taken a skydiving experience every time he'd kissed her. She'd spun out of control and still felt that way. She hadn't been able to concentrate the last few days. Her mind was constantly on him, and though she had looked out the window in the dark hours of the night and seen him sitting there, she'd stayed away. She didn't trust herself to not throw herself at him.

And she couldn't do that. Though she knew that she was falling for her neighbor faster than she'd believed possible she also knew that something bothered him and he hadn't shared anything personal about his past with her. Not that they'd actually spent all that much time together, not in the big realm of things. And today he'd turned down spending time with her in her dynamite dress and instead chose to scrape paint off shutters. How exciting was that? And what did that say about any feelings she'd thought he might be having toward her after he'd rocked her world with his kisses?

It was a blow that she was finding hard to find any joy in. But she wasn't about to let anyone know this. She plastered on her smile and lavished love on Clarence and Belva and all the other residents of the retirement home. She ignored that her heart was suddenly wanting things that she had thought she wasn't ready for. Not yet. But all it had taken was a few days, a very few short weeks spent knowing Adam, to change that.

The wedding was lovely, and she was sitting in the back row of chairs with tears of joy in her eyes when someone sat down in the chair beside her and held a tissue close to her face.

"Don't cry," that familiar masculine voice whispered close to her ear and sent tingles flowing through her like lava.

She took the tissue, her fingers touching his as she did so, and her heart jangled in her chest. "You came. I thought you had shutters to clean?"

"I'm an idiot. Why would I want to clean shutters when I could come here and dance with the most beautiful and special woman in the world?"

Startled by his words, she faltered to find words. "Um, well, that's pushing things a good bit. But I'm so glad you're here."

He tilted her chin and looked into her eyes with such intensity that she almost lost her voice. "You are to me."

Her breath just whooshed out of her as if an elephant had sat on her chest, and she got lost in his eyes. No one had ever looked at her like that.

And then he took her hand and kissed it.

Feeling shaken, she held his hand and forced her gaze back to the older couple as they recited their vows; then, holding hands, they kissed. It was beautiful and she loved that love could be found at any age. *Had she found it?*

Her heart said yes but her common sense made her take a step back and keep an open perspective.

Feeling self-conscious, a few moments later she led the way to the reception table and helped cut the cake and hand out dishes of strawberry delight muffins to everyone. Adam helped her, taking plates of the dessert to the residents in wheelchairs and making sure they had punch, too.

"That is such a good man. With a good heart," Mami said, coming to help with the cake duties. "I hoped he might come to dance with you."

"Yes, he is. But I think he came to dance with you." She winked at Mami as he came their way. He had come to the wedding and sat beside her and kissed her hand but she was not going to jump to any conclusions. Wrong conclusions could hurt. And besides that, she still wasn't sure about what she wanted out of this. And yet when his eyes met hers, she felt as if someone had turned the heaters on and the place was going to explode into flames.

It was a little bit scary. In a really good way.

And her grateful clock was spinning out of control.

"It's time to get the dancing started," Clarence boomed from the middle of the room. "I'm ready to dance with my beautiful bride."

"Oh Clarence, you are such a charmer." Belva slipped her hand into the one he held out to her, and as if the recreation director had been waiting for her cue, she punched a button and "Unforgettable" began playing.

"Isn't that beautiful," Rosie said when Adam came to stand next to her, their shoulders touching.

"It is. I'm glad you invited me."

She was too.

When the next song started, the older couples paired up and began dancing to "Smoke Gets In My Eyes," another oldie that Adam loved. He turned to Rosie. "May I have this dance?"

Her eyes were wide, and for a moment, he saw a vulnerability in their depths that he hadn't seen before. When she placed her hand in his, he could almost feel the racing of her heart as it matched the pace of his. Slipping his hand around her waist, he led her onto the dance floor. She fit into his arms as if she'd been made for him, and as the romantic song played, he lost himself in the feel of her in his arms. He'd been right in coming. He'd needed this. He was more grateful to

Tate than his brother would ever know, for his words that had helped him see more clearly.

The day had been magical, and now Rosie was riding home with Adam. "Thank you for the ride home," she said, as soon as the truck came to a halt next to their cottages. Her heart skipped lightly as he placed a hand on her arm.

"Don't get out just yet. Just sit right there."

Confused and her skin burning where he'd touched her, she sat and waited as he got out of the truck, strode around the truck, and opened the door for her. He held his hand out for her and she slipped her hand into his. Her cheeks flushed, as was becoming the norm where he was concerned. In the late afternoon light, she could have let her mind waltz through romantic notions about them. They'd danced several dances together with over forty chaperones dancing around them and then he'd danced with as many of the ladies as he could get to while she was practically swept off her feet by every older gentleman resident who could stand. And some in wheelchairs. Mami had done her fair share of dancing too.

It was a wonderful wedding and every time her gaze met Adam's, his eyes crinkled around the edges and his lips quirked into a smile, as if they shared a private link between just the two of them. They'd needed Lila there to help, but her family had been in for the weekend, and Doreen had been out of town too or just used that as an excuse because she was too shy. And Birdie had another commitment, so that had left just poor Mami to help her host. And Adam. Once again, he'd come to her rescue.

Now his eyes crinkled and he held her hand securely as she slid from the seat to stand next to him. He stared at her, and she stared up at him. The tension that had been wound so tight between them all the way from the Sandy Shores Retirement Home cranked tighter. Rosie lifted her free hand and placed it on his heart, because he was still holding her other hand in his, in midair as if frozen there. His heart thundered beneath her touch and she wanted this man to kiss her again. To pull her close and have a repeat of the kiss he'd given her on Saturday.

And then he did. He slid his arm around her, pulled her in close and lowered his lips to hers. And Rosie was lost in the feel of being in Adam's embrace, lost in the feel of his lips working magic over hers and causing a yearning to rage through her that she'd never, ever felt before. It was building with each kiss they shared.

But this time, she knew that the world as she knew it had just changed forever.

CHAPTER FIFTEEN

Adam had issues to overcome. He told himself this even as he lowered his head and kissed Rosie. It was as if he'd lost his mind. Or his heart.

She'd been like an angel at that wedding, fluttering around and making sure it was a beautiful day for the wedding couple and the guests. And when he'd arrived late, he'd stood at the back of the room at first and watched as she sat in the back row, dabbing at her eyes without tissues. She'd been touched by the wedding even before the preacher started the ceremony. He'd felt a strong compulsion to sweep her off her feet and ask her to marry him right there in the back row. It was as if something had taken him over and he wasn't using his head.

He was a planner. A contemplator. Especially on important matters. Unless he was in the trauma unit, where his skill, his mind, and his gut became one and instinct took over. Standing there with that instinct telling him that Rosie was the love of his life, he knew in his heart of hearts that what Tate had said was true. He'd wanted Mikie to live and he'd given everything he had to give to make it so...but time hadn't been on his side. And nothing he did could have turned back the clock to give him that time.

As much as Mikie's death hurt, there was freedom for Adam in this assurance. His death hadn't been because Adam had been too tired or burned out. He kissed Rosie with relief, with passion and a sense of hope. Hope that if he played his cards right, her brand of sunshine could fill his days for the rest of his life.

Lifting his head, he stared down into her dazzling eyes. "Rosie, will you take a walk on the beach with me?"

"I'd like that."

She stepped out of her heels; he bent and picked them up and placed them in the seat of his truck. Then he removed his dress shoes and socks, and set them beside hers. He rolled his pants up to his ankles and then closed the door and took her hand again. They walked across the white sugar sand toward the topaz water.

His heart hammered, but he'd never felt more right about anything in his life with Rosie beside him. They walked silently down the wet sand as they'd done several times before, each time special.

A little down the beach, a man was fishing and a pelican was trying to steal his bait.

Adam laughed. "Looks like Seymour is back and causing trouble."

"Looks that way. I'm not sure where he's been off to but it's good to see him return. I will never forget seeing you that first day, fussing with that pelican."

"I'm sure it was a sight. I'll never forget looking up and finding you standing there." He turned and took her hands. "Rosie, it was like a bolt of lightning to my life when I first saw you standing there. You were a ray of sunlight shining bright at a time when I needed a ray of sunshine. A ray of hope. I was about as low as I've ever been when I first came back here. I haven't even been able to talk about it. Until today."

"Adam. I'm so sorry. I knew you were struggling with something."

His lips flattened together and he nodded, gathering the will to speak. "I lost a patient I thought I should have been able to save. I wanted to save him…Mikie. His name was Mikie and he was only ten. But there was no time." He raked a hand through his hair, wanting to pull it out. "I've blamed myself, thought because I was burned out that I might have not had the time to save him because I was reacting slow. My brother Tate came by right after you and Mami left and he helped me realize that it wasn't me—there was just no time left by the time Mikie was brought in to me. Poor boy didn't have a chance. But I've been questioning myself ever since that day, and grieving too. I can't imagine what his family is going through. They blamed me and that has haunted me too, made me question myself even more. But, they were grieving and lashed out. I understand."

Rosie wrapped her arms around his waist and hugged him. And he let the feel of her warm him.

She pulled back and looked up at him with a mixture of fire and sympathy. "Adam, you listen to me. I know you too. And I have seen you in action on things of far less importance than saving a precious child's life or any life, and I can assure you that you go all in on everything. Do you hear me? You give everything, and I mean everything, you've got to every task. Even baking muffins. Or cleaning up afterward. And then the way you touch people with kindness…there is no question in my mind that you did everything you could to save that little boy."

Her words enveloped him, filled him up.

She cupped his face, smoothing her thumb across his skin, and he knew…knew his heart was not wrong in what it felt for this woman. "Your confidence means a lot to me. You mean a lot to me, Rosie. I don't want to scare you away but I'm falling head over heels in love with you. I can't get you off my mind. And I don't want to. You make me see things in a new light. Your kindness warms me. Your light draws me. Feeds me. That's why I can't get you off my mind. Or my heart."

Her eyes grew as large as a huge sand dollar. "Adam Sinclair, I hate to break it to you but I think I lost my heart to you the night you drove me home from spending all day making muffins for the festival. Right there, sitting in our driveway."

His heart expanded, and light and joy ignited within him. "I don't know what to say." And then he didn't say anything because she wrapped her arms around his neck and she kissed him…and he decided that words could wait.

Later, looking very satisfied with herself, Rosie pulled back from kissing him and smiled. "There. That, for your information, was the first time *I've* ever kissed a man. I've experienced a lot of firsts with you."

His head was spinning and his knees were weak. "I have to say that I thought since you'd never been kissed until the day on the beach when I kissed you, that you'd never kissed a man either. And I need to let you know that you did a mighty fine job of it, being that you haven't had any practice."

She got an impish expression. "A fine job? Oh no, fine won't do. I need to do a *great* job. Practice makes perfect—"

He placed two fingers over her lips. "Hold on. I need to say something first."

And right there, on the spur of the moment, Adam dropped to his knee.

"W-what are you doing?" Rosie whispered, her voice trembling.

Adam had never felt more certain of anything in his life. "Rosie Olsen, will you marry me and practice kissing me for the rest of our lives?"

Her eyes were huge and they slowly filled with tears as she stared down at him in shock. Or maybe she'd lost her voice—and he suspected that had never happened before. Another first in her life.

He smiled up at her. "Are you going to answer? Or are you speechless?"

Rosie couldn't speak. Her heart thundered in her chest as Rosie stared down at Adam. Unable to speak or think or believe this was actually happening. She'd dreamed of forever and thought it was out of her grasp. Thought she'd leave this earth without having experienced a forever kind of love. Then Adam had entered her life. And she'd begun to hope.

She dropped to her knees in front of him. "Yes," she whispered, then more forcefully, "Yes!" Leaning into him, she kissed him and he pulled her closer as their hearts beat as one. Adam returned the kiss, leaving her breathless with feelings she'd never felt before. Their kiss turned passionate and she very literally felt swept away with a host of emotions and new feelings.

When she came up for air, she pulled back to look at him. His eyes held hers. "I think I have a lot to learn."

He chuckled huskily. "I think we both do. But we'll take it slow and not get ahead of ourselves. I want to marry you, Rosie Olsen."

"I think slow is good. But Adam, this is right."

He cupped her face. "This is very right. And I'm the luckiest man alive."

Rosie nearly cried as he tenderly kissed her with the promise of everything she'd ever dared to hope and dream of and her happy tears were because she was so thankful to have lived to feel his love.

CHAPTER SIXTEEN

"So, what do you girls think?" Rosie had waited until Mami, Birdie, Lila, and Doreen were all seated at their table by the window before she carried their coffee and muffins over. It was Tuesday morning and she had something wonderful to show them. She held out her left hand with its princess cut solitaire sparkling on her ring finger.

"*That*—that is an engagement ring," Lila exclaimed, shoving her glasses higher on her nose to get a better look.

"Oh my, that good-looking rascal proposed,"

Mami declared. "I knew it the moment he took you in his arms at that wedding that he was a goner. And a smart fella."

"I never doubted him for a minute," Birdie huffed. "He knew a good thing when he saw it."

"It's so romantic." Doreen teared up, looking at the ring, then up at Rosie. "You two make a perfect couple. Congratulations."

"Thank you. Thank you all. I am so happy. He's the most wonderful man and I can't wait to start my life with him." Rosie still could not believe how her life had changed over the weekend. Over the last few weeks. How had it happened? It was still almost a mystery to her that the blessing of love rained down on her like it had. She had been longing for forever for, well, forever, and now she was going to marry the man of her dreams.

"So, how did he do it?" Lila beamed at Rosie. "And how does he kiss? I bet he knows how." Lila's mouth dropped open in a gaping smile and she hitched her brows up, making a very hilarious look.

Rosie chuckled. "You're right about that, Lila—he

can kiss. Very well. You would approve."

"Me too," Mami said. "I thought he could from the first moment he strode in here looking all manly and strong. He had me at hello." She hooted with laughter.

"Me too," Doreen said, her smile enhanced by the rose of her cheeks.

"He had me when I saw him working without his shirt on," Birdie said. "But it was Rosie we wanted to see the light. Did he drop to his knee or did he sweep you off your feet? Don't dawdle—give us the details."

Rosie laughed at the sweet ladies. "Actually, Birdie, he did both. He swept me off my feet the moment I met him and then Saturday after the wedding, completely a surprise, he kissed me and then knelt and asked me to marry him."

"Oh, just like a romance movie." Doreen had cupped her hands together. "It's just so sweet."

"Yes, it is. When's the wedding?" Birdie asked. The others leaned forward in anticipation.

"We haven't set the date yet. I'm not sure yet. We're surprising his family tonight with the news. I'm hoping you ladies can keep this a secret at least until six when I'll be with Adam at his mother and dad's home, telling everyone."

"We can keep the secret until six," Mami said, her eyes twinkling. "But not a moment longer."

"That's right," Lila said. "When the clock strikes six, we are going to crow like roosters crowing at the sunrise."

Rosie's heart warmed and she shook her head. "You ladies are a mess. Give me till six o'clock and then you can shout it from the rooftops."

"Don't think we won't," Birdie huffed.

She chuckled and held her ring out so she could see it sparkle in the overhead light. "Oh, I'm fairly certain you might. You do whatever makes you happy. Because I know I plan to."

And that was the truth.

Adam led Rosie into his parents' home. They were intentionally running late because he hadn't wanted to get there before everyone else arrived, wanting to let them all in on their surprise at the same time. Tate wasn't going to be there because he'd already left for his assignment, so Adam had called and told him the news. Tate had been thrilled for him and taken credit for the match because he had sent Adam to the muffin shop. Adam didn't bother reminding him that Rosie was his neighbor and they'd already met before he went to the Bake My Day bakery—and it had literally made his day and his life.

Rosie was nervous; he could feel her hand tremble in his as they walked into the kitchen to find the room full of his family. His parents, Erin, Brad, and Jonah had made it on time and Cassie was back in town and here too.

All the people he loved in one room. Except Tate, but he was here in spirit.

His mother's eyes widened and she instantly stepped forward. "And you must be Rosie," she said, coming to them.

"Yes, ma'am, I am."

"I have been dying to meet you. It took all my willpower not to come to the bakery and spy on you the moment I heard Adam was interested. But I was afraid if I met you I'd want to meddle and I might ruin a good thing. It is wonderful to have you here. I'm Maryetta and this is my husband Leo, Adam's father."

"It's so nice to meet you both." Rosie shined a bright smile at them.

He saw speculation and anticipation in both of his parents' expressions.

Brad winked at her. "My men love Rosie's muffins. She's dropped some by the firehouse and now my men think they need to be part of the budget. They're delicious. They almost fought over the ones I got the day of the festival."

"I'm glad," Rosie said.

"I think your bakery is the new hot spot in town," Erin broke in, coming close to give Rosie a hug. "It's amazingly great to have you here. With Adam," she said, her eyes sparkling as they welcomed Rosie. Then she spoke to the family, turning slightly and taking them all in with her gaze. "Rosie's muffins are a huge hit with my guests. I've put an order in with her ever since I opened for guests last month and they are devoured. The residents of Sunset Bay know a good thing when they see it. Obviously, our brother does too." She elbowed Brad. "This one missed the boat."

Brad winked. "Not meant to be."

"Sounds like I'm missing out. I'm Cassie, and I've been so busy these last few months that I've barely had time to do anything other than work. But I'll make it a priority to get by and have a cup of coffee and a muffin. I'm really glad you're here."

"Me, too. I'm Jonah. Adam will have to bring you down to the boat dock and take you out on the water."

"Jonah owns Jonah's Boat Rental & Storage," Adam said.

"Oh, the one with the logo of the whale spitting the cute caricature out of his mouth. I think that's a really cute logo." Rosie beamed.

His brother laughed. "Yep, that's me. My name and my business were too much of a coincidence for me to pass up on the logo."

"It's very catchy."

"Bake My Day is, too. I'd have come by but I'm not much of a sweets eater. But I do drink coffee so I'll have to stop in."

Erin elbowed him. "He's actually afraid to come in. He's afraid he'll be tempted by all those delicious treats and start eating them and be unable to stop. Might mess up his washboard abs."

Jonah shook his head in patient denial, scratched the back of his neck and looked embarrassed. "Not exactly true."

Cassie grinned and joined Erin in teasing their quieter brother. "Maybe the part about you eating all the muffins. But the abs are definitely true." She looked at Rosie. "All my brothers have been blessed with lean, muscled bods while I have to fight with every calorie I even look at to keep these curves at least a little under control." She waved a hand down her fuller figure. "It's just not fair.

"Tell me about it," Erin said, patting her own flat stomach. "I have to jog every day I can find a spare moment."

"Hey, we exercise too." Brad looked insulted.

"But you can eat anything you want with no worries." Erin didn't let him off the hook.

Everyone laughed because it was true. Brad ate anything and everything he wanted, but his lifestyle was active. It took a lot of fuel to energize his big frame. Adam and Jonah were built slimmer than Brad and Tate but they had all inherited a lean frame from their dad. Erin had the body of a runner while Cassie had always had a curvier figure that Adam knew had never bothered his friends. In high school he'd had to warn many a boy that if he got out of line with either of his sisters they'd have all four of the Sinclair brothers to deal with. The girls hadn't been happy with them for their interference.

"I think you look lovely," Rosie said, sweetly. "But if you're serious I have options. I have muffins and pastries that fit in with all types of eating needs. I can't stand the idea of someone coming in and seeing my pretty lovelies and not being able to have one."

"I think that's wonderful and thoughtful," his mother said, looking happily on as Rosie got to know his family.

Adam felt pride and love tangle in his chest watching Rosie with everyone. He put his arm around her and tugged her close to his side, contentment filling him. He knew this was right. "Everyone, we have something to share."

His mother's eyes crinkled at the edges and she looked at him with a mixture of hope and disbelief. He smiled, and gave a short laugh of joy. Yes, joy. He'd felt that joy from the moment he'd met Rosie, but since she'd said yes to marrying him, it was overflowing. And now, soon, his mother would have her wish.

"I've asked Rosie to marry me and she accepted."

The room erupted in exclamations of congratulations. His mother's mouth dropped open momentarily, as if too stunned to believe it.

"I am so happy," she said after a second and threw her arms around him and Rosie. "Welcome to our family, Rosie." She pulled back and cupped Rosie's cheeks. "I've been waiting on you for a very long time."

Rosie's smile was infectious as she looked at his mom and took in her words. "Perfect, because I am so glad to be here. I love your son so very much."

"That is music to this mother's ears."

"And this father's. I'm really happy, too. I could tell Adam had something on his mind last week and now I know what it was. It was you. Congratulations."

"We have a lot to talk about," Maryetta said,

delight emanating from her. "We have a wedding to plan. Our first wedding. Oh my goodness I can hardly believe it. Do you have a ring?"

"I do." Rosie had turned the engagement ring so that the stone was hidden on the palm side of her hand, and now she twisted it so that it shone proudly for all to see. Instantly the women in his family went into dreamy mode, oohing and cooing over the ring while his brothers and his dad clapped him on his back.

Brad leaned in and whispered, "Thanks, man, for taking the pressure off the rest of us. We owe you big time for this."

Adam looked toward Rosie. "You don't owe me anything. I'm taking this one for the team because it's the best thing that's ever happened to me in my life. And I want to."

He met Brad's gaze, realizing there was a distance there, a shadow, and he worried then that maybe his brother was feeling more than he was showing. Was his own past of rejection and betrayal bringing that look there? Brad quickly covered it with a ready smile.

"I'm glad. You deserve it."

And you don't? The question tugged at Adam. Did

Brad think he didn't deserve happiness like this? Adam looked back at Rosie, knowing how that had felt, knowing he hadn't felt deserving of it after all that had happened in his life over the last months. And he knew with all his heart and soul that Rosie was the best thing that had ever happened to him.

As if she heard his thoughts, Rosie turned to look at him. Their gazes locked and he saw his future. She smiled, her special smile meant for him alone and he knew he was the luckiest man alive.

He reached for her and she came willingly, and then with all of his family watching he kissed her with all the tenderness welling up inside of him. "How did I ever live without your love? I love you, Rosie."

"I'm so glad you found me. I've been longing for you forever."

Joy and love shone in her eyes, filling him up and making him whole. "And I feel the same."

And it was true, everything he'd ever longed for was right here, wrapped up in Rosie's love.

Forever.

EPILOGUE

Brad got into his Jeep after leaving the family dinner. He gripped the steering wheel and told his heart to stop racing. He'd felt the love overflowing between Adam and Rosie and an ache he'd thought he'd finally overcome welled up inside of him. He sat there for a moment, trying to gather his wits. Struggling with the emotions assaulting him.

Putting the Jeep in reverse, he checked the rearview, then punched the gas and backed out of the driveway feeling as if his world was spinning out of control. He had to shake this. He had to get past this crazy storm of emotions that held him tangled in its vortex ever since Katie had walked out on him.

He rammed the gearshift into drive and drove away, leaving his parents' home behind. Adam and Rosie didn't deserve his sorry attitude bringing down their happy moment. Not that they knew he felt this way. He was really, really good at hiding the storm inside of him.

He drove straight through town, passing the firehouse and the dog park, spotting a flash of red hair. His thoughts instantly went back to Katie, with her pretty mass of auburn hair and tall, sleek, athletic body that had enabled her and him to enjoy all the outdoor hikes and climbs and activity that had always connected them in so many ways.

Two years had passed since she'd taken the dreams he'd planned for them most of his life and ripped his heart out by suddenly marrying someone else. He'd been completely and totally blindsided. Wiped out.

It had been a fast fall to hell for him and tonight he'd learned with shocking clarity that he hadn't made it out yet. Not even close.

After she'd left he'd been a mess, then he'd thrown himself into dating every female who showed interest. He'd joked, teased, and lived it up. None of the dates had lasted but that hadn't stopped him from continuing his merry-go-round dating. Staying home alone was just not an option.

And then he'd gotten the Fire Chief job and that had helped him cope and discontinue some of his reckless behavior. His job kept him busy and required him to be more responsible. He'd dated less, which was still a lot, while secretly he hoped that somewhere out there someone would wipe the memory of Katie from his heart.

Not that he planned to ever fall in love again because much to his mother's sorrow, though she didn't know it yet, he didn't have plans to ever give anyone enough leverage on his heart to hurt him like that again.

He needed time alone, to get his head clear and to face down the jealousy that he'd felt at Adam's happiness. He was glad for Adam, just envious that his own fairytale hadn't come true.

He glanced in his rearview, searching for the flash of red hair somewhere behind him, then he yanked his gaze back to the road and continued heading out of town. He'd always loved red hair and could still remember the feel of Katie's hair as he'd run his fingers through that thick mane. He'd thought he would be ruined on the color, but no, he found himself continually drawn to that vibrant color. Maybe it was because he was a fireman and he was trained to run toward the fire. To run into the flames. But he'd been burned, and despite the fact that he found himself many times dating other redheads, he had no plans to ever get burned again.

Reaching the dirt road that led down to the secluded beach, he eased on the brake and then took the turn faster than he should have as his wheels hit the off-road track. Might as well put the off-road Jeep to the test.

A few minutes later he drove from the road onto the sand and pulled to a halt at the dunes just as his phone buzzed. Being the fire chief and first responder, he automatically accepted the call. "Sinclair," he said.

"Brad, are you okay?"

He inhaled hard at the sound of Adam's voice. "Sure am. What's up, soon-to-be newlywed?" he asked, forcing his voice to hold the natural good-natured teasing that had been one of his saving graces through all of this. Even down and out he generally enjoyed life.

"I happened to follow you outside. I had a question for you, but you were already driving away and you looked upset."

He normally kept his pain carefully locked behind his smile. He'd barely gotten out of the house tonight. The wedding announcement had been a surprise. The undying love radiating between Adam and Rosie had been like a gut punch to him.

"I'm fine. I'm really happy for you two."

"Thanks, but, are you sure you're okay? I got to thinking that this might have brought back bad memories."

Adam hadn't been here during the time when Katie had left him, but he and Adam had always been close and he'd broken down and called Adam one night when he'd been going through a particularly hard time. "I'm fine. Well, maybe not as good as I want to pretend. Seeing you and Rosie so happy brings back how I once felt. Kind of opened up a wound. But I'll get over it. I'm really happy for you." He meant it, really. He meant it with all of his own doomed heart.

"Thanks, that means a lot to me."

"What did you want to ask me?"

"I wanted to ask you if you'd be my best man? Tate and Jonah are going to be groomsmen, but I'd be honored if you would be best man."

His stomach lurched and he closed his eyes as conflicting emotions collided. He didn't want this. Wasn't sure how he'd feel standing up there. "I'd be honored." The words came out stiff. "If you're sure you want me."

"I do."

His mouth was dry as he nodded, then realized he needed to say something. "Then I'll be there for you. Anything you need, I'm there for you."

"That means a lot to me. And same here. I'll let

you go, thanks again."

The line went dead and he dropped his phone into the seat and climbed from the Jeep. He jogged to the beach and stopped just short of where the waves could get his running shoes wet. He raked his hands through his hair and lifted his face to the evening light. He had to move on.

"I have to," he said aloud, as if hearing the words spoken would make him move on.

As much as he was reluctant to be anywhere near a wedding, maybe if he made it through it he could leave his own bad past behind.

He didn't like wallowing. He'd never been a wallowing kind of guy and he didn't like himself much right now.

Turning away, he headed back to his Jeep just as his alarm went off.

Fire.

That was his signal to roll. In seconds, he had the county dispatcher on his emergency phone to get the lowdown. A fire was in an apartment complex just off of Seashell and Starfish. The complex was just down the street from Bake My Day off Seashell and Main, his future sister-in-law's coffee shop.

Time to work. He hit the gas as soon as his tires touched pavement. He was barking orders into the phone as he drove. There were people in the building counting on him and his crew to get them out.

And he didn't plan on letting any of them down today. No matter how down he was in his own life, people were depending on him.

Excerpt from

LONGING FOR A HERO

Sunset Bay Romance, Book Two

CHAPTER ONE

Lulu Raintree started out of the dog park, struggling to control Sebastian, a large, hairy, white beauty that was a mixture of breeds and a playful handful. She had just gotten the gate opened and stepped out onto the sidewalk when the all too familiar Jeep came into her view.

Fire Chief Brad Sinclair.

The instant she saw him in the driver's seat, her gaze locked onto him like a heat-seeking missile. He looked upset. As if her gaze drew his attention, he looked her way. She jumped back behind the bush, tripped over Sebastian, and toppled backward over him. She landed with a hard thud on the grass next to the concrete sidewalk, with her feet straight up in the air. Sebastian, thinking she was playing, pounced on her, dancing on her chest and barking as if he were king of the mountain.

"Sebastian." She laughed, mortified that Brad might have witnessed her clumsiness and grateful that the big brute of a dog had helped to cover her up so that now there was a chance that the gorgeous fire chief might not have seen her at all.

Pushing Sebastian off her and hugging him, she rolled to her knees and peeked to make sure the Jeep was long gone. It was. The coast was clear. Dusting herself off, she headed in the opposite direction from Brad. Sunset Bay wasn't a huge beach town, but like most, it was long and left ample room to avoid someone if you really wanted to. And she wanted to avoid the man who drove all her good sense out the window just by the mere essence of his presence.

Then again, there was the fact that she was a dog

walker. At least, here in her new life in Sunset Bay, she was a dog walker. That hadn't always been the case. But as a dog walker, the fact that the dog park was across the street from the fire station did pose problems.

She was glad there hadn't been any other dog walkers in the park to witness her topple. She rubbed Sebastian on the head. "Okay, you really have a problem," she muttered. Sebastian turned his head and planted his big eyes on her. "Not you—me. I know you know it. I talk to you about it enough."

It was true. Her dogs were good listeners. No one else knew her history but she often found herself telling her doggy clients her troubles. Her fears and her hopes.

As she contemplated her life and in general her weirdness, Sebastian yanked and strained at the end of the leash the moment he spotted a squirrel. She had to leave her thoughts behind and hold onto the dog with all her might. He loved to chase squirrels and when the nearly sixty-pound pooch saw something he wanted, he went for it. Lulu was short, carried a few extra pounds on her hips and had a weakness for fresh baked muffins, so she had an ongoing battle with the scales and it was hard for her to sometimes keep up with the powerful single-minded dog.

Half the time, Sebastian drug her around town at the end of his leash instead of her walking him. It was no different this afternoon. As they were getting their walk in, she couldn't get Brad Sinclair off her mind. She had to do something about her reactions to the man.

What if someone had been watching her comedy act earlier when she saw him and then flipped backward over Sebastian and ended up on the ground? Rosie Olsen had spotted her hiding behind the Korney Korn truck during the town festival a couple of weeks ago. She saw Lulu peeking from behind the trailer but Rosie hadn't known what she was doing. She had wondered, though, and Lulu was sure Rosie had believed she was acting strange.

Of course, anyone would probably understand her actions if they knew it was Brad Sinclair who caused her reactions.

But that didn't change her confusion at those reactions to him. Or how foolish she felt.

The man was a walking heartthrob and a heartache to her. Just the sight of him sent her heart slamming into her throat. Her knees had nearly buckled as she'd watched him pass by and, honestly, it was ridiculous that she, as a grown woman, felt the need to break out and run after his Jeep. Thankfully, she'd tripped over the dog instead.

The man drove her crazy. In a crazy way.

She had an almost unhealthy crush on him. She tried to avoid him at all costs because she was a bumbling klutz when he was around. So embarrassing.

Once, she'd had the unfortunate situation in a restaurant that she referred to as the great shrimp fiasco and could not bring herself to be anywhere around him where he would recognize her. And yet, she came to the dog park across from the firehouse every day to let the dogs run free and play. She hid behind the large bush in the dog park so she was out of view, and yet, she could glimpse him every day. A problem—big-time—yes, it was. And she wasn't sure how to fix it, because she didn't completely understand it. She'd moved to Sunset Bay to get over heartbreak…real, true heartbreak so why had she immediately become infatuated with Brad Sinclair? She just didn't understand her heart. Or herself for that matter. She had a problem and there was no denying the fact.

The salted air ruffled Fire Chief Brad Sinclair's hair and stung his eyes as, emergency lights flashing and siren screaming, he sped down the coastal road back toward Sunset Bay. He had been at his parents' home for dinner and not driven the red SUV supplied by the county. His personal vehicle was set up for him to respond to emergencies also and he'd wanted the open-air Jeep tonight. After his brother, Adam, had sprung a sudden engagement to the owner of Bake My Day bakery on the family, he'd needed the Jeep and the blast of fresh air as soon as he'd been able to wish them well and make his escape to the outskirts of town and a secluded stretch of beach. No sooner than he'd arrived Adam had called him, having seen him leave and looking upset. Something he hadn't wanted anyone to see. And then Adam had asked him to be best man.

Best man.

He was really happy for Adam, and he was now supposed to be his best man and he wasn't sure he could do it.

Just because two years ago the love of his life literally ripped his heart out and ran off to marry someone else didn't mean he was supposed to be brokenhearted for the rest of his life. But the way it was going, he feared he might be. Despite the fact that he hid it well with a lot of dates, a lot of smiling, and work, nothing seemed to ease his pain.

Work saved him. His work as fire chief was important. People counted on him. That kept him focused for the most part. It didn't cure the pain, the feelings of rejection, or fill the hole. But it helped.

As the plume of smoke in the air grew closer and the town came into view, he shoved the thoughts from his mind. He was almost there, meaning no room for thoughts of his past while he was working. His work required his full attention.

People counted on him and despite the fact that he'd suffered a letdown didn't mean he was letting anyone down.

About an hour after spotting Brad, Lulu was across town and still thinking about the man. Whether she wanted to or not. He was just there, stuck in her head. Taking up space she really didn't need him taking up.

He'd looked upset when he'd passed her earlier, though. What had been wrong with him?

She, like everyone in town, knew the story of his love for his childhood sweetheart and that they'd planned to marry and then she'd run off with someone else, leaving him brokenhearted—boy did she know how that felt. It was hard to see that the happy, dashing man who dated gorgeous women and rescued people from burning buildings sad. And she knew he was despite the brave face he showed the world. Of course, that was her take on him. He pretty much wore the red cape of a superhero where she was concerned. Just last week when she was walking Spaz and Sussi-Q the most terribly mannered terriers in the world, to put it in polite terms, she spotted him actually climbing a tree to save a kitty for a little girl. He had been completely adorable...the little girl had been too. But Brad, well he had stolen the show. She'd hidden behind Mr.

Womack's plumbing truck and had been thankful that the terriers were trying to sniff out a mole that was tunneling a trail along the edge of the lawn. Her only problem had been when they found it and started straining at the end of their leashes and barking their cute little dirt covered heads off with excitement. Brad had been halfway down the tree with the kitty snuggled in his arms and had looked in her direction. She'd had to pick the pups up and make a dash for the edge of the house before he spotted her.

Yes, the man was a hero, and not just to kittens and little girls. He'd busted down a door to Mildred and Roland Birches home and he and Dex, one of the other firemen, had carried them out. That was just a few of the instances that he'd been a real life hero. But the truth was that he and the other firemen were ready to put their lives on the line to protect the people of this town from fire and disasters. And that was where the trouble for her started. There were plenty of heroes in town, from military veterans to firefighters to the police. There were more she was certain and the only one she had this infatuation with was Brad Sinclair.

She was biting her lip and letting Sebastian lead

her as they passed the firehouse. It was quiet there and she'd kept her head down. She hadn't gone a hundred feet when the sirens sounded and she spotted the plume of smoke rising in the late afternoon sky toward her and Sebastian's apartments on the other side of town. Moments later, the largest of the three Sunset Bay firetrucks barreled down Seashell Lane and sent Sebastian into a fit of excitement. Yanking at his leash, the dog took off, chasing the firetruck and practically dragging her behind him. Of course, the firetrucks left them behind instantly but that didn't stop the dog from acting wildly out of control. Way out of control even for him.

She barely held onto the leash as she struggled to get her short legs to keep up with him. "Stop, Sebastian," she called. "Stop. Stay. Halt. *W-whoa—*" She struggled block after block but the dog would not calm down.

She was winded but hanging on, running madly down the center lane of the oddly deserted street as the last block before her apartment complex came into view and she realized that was what was on fire.

Was the dog out of control because it had sensed it

the moment the firetrucks went by?

Now, with the firetrucks and apartments and people standing around in sight, Sebastian completely lost it. She did too, and, gasping, pushed harder to follow along as they raced toward the fire.

The scene of the fire at Starfish Manor was chaotic as, sirens blaring, the backup pumper truck pulled to a halt next to Brad's Jeep. The first-floor apartment that had been engulfed in flames when they'd been called had been contained. He'd just come out from his initial look and he suspected an electrical problem had started the fire. No one had been in the apartment and his men were checking all the apartments to make sure everyone was safe.

People swarmed everywhere, not knowing what to do. He'd gotten everyone to move back and barriers were put up as the men had gone into the burning building.

He was thankful the fire was contained to one floor and the call had come quickly so they could arrive before it had spread. Though the barrier was up, residents were worried as his men made sure the fire was contained. He was having a conversation with his hose man when suddenly a dog barking wildly drew his attention to the street. A large white dog barreled past the pumper truck, towing a small red-haired woman behind him. The woman clung to the dog's leash, yelling for the canine to stop. But it was doing no good. The dog was determined and had no intention of stopping until it reached its destination.

"That doesn't look so good." Dex Carpenter stepped to the side to stare.

Brad slapped his clipboard to Dex's chest. "Here, hold this. Someone needs to stop that runaway train." He could see the wide eyes on the redhead and knew that the dog was leading her straight into the path of his men. Although the fire hadn't been anywhere near as bad as it could have been, he still didn't need this disaster getting in their way. Besides that, it was clear the woman needed help. That dog was almost as big as she was. He took six steps and intercepted the dog.

But it didn't go exactly as he'd planned. The massive dog dodged him, and the woman slammed into him; his arms wound around her and they both flew backward and hit the ground with a thud. Her gasp of pain registered as he took the hit on his back and she landed on top of him. And where the dog went was momentarily forgotten.

"I'll get the dog, Chief," Dex yelled as Brad lay sprawled across the grass with a mass of red hair covering his face and the fresh scent of fruity watermelon momentarily distracted him from the smell of smoke.

"Are you okay?" He felt her heart pounding against his, and liked the soft feel of her in his arms.

"I-I think," she stuttered. Her head lifted from his shoulder to reveal an oval-shaped face, with clear green eyes that stared at him with bewilderment through the threads of her auburn hair. In the seconds that their gazes locked, her gaze went from bewilderment to shock; then her pretty pink mouth opened and her eyes filled with horror. "It's you. Oh, no. Oh, I am so sorry." She scrambled to get off of him and when that didn't happen fast enough she pretty much crawled three feet away from him, muttering to herself then popping to her feet, all barely five feet of her.

From there she glared wide-eyed at him—pretty much as if she'd just had a run in with a snake or a skunk.

Stunned by her reaction to him, he'd released her and watched her frantic escape. Concerned for her and not sure what was going on he sat up. "Are you alright?" he asked, just as Dex showed up, holding the leash of the dog.

"Got him," Dex said.

The dog woofed and dove on top of Brad. One minute, he'd had an intriguing soft woman in his arms and the next, he had the hairy mass of a brute dog dancing all over him. And all while he was trying to figure out what had caused the look of horror on Green-eyes face. He'd seen her around town, just not close up very much. Once.

"No, Sebastian, no!" Green-eyes gasped. She reached to wrap her arms around the dog's neck and pull it off him.

Brad pushed and Dex pulled on the leash, and together they got the out-of-control animal off him long enough for Brad to get to a standing position.

From beyond the barrier, someone screamed the

dog's name and came running up. It was a woman in her fifties, wearing a suit.

"Thank goodness, he's all right," she wailed, reaching them and throwing her arms around the dog. It instantly became a new dog and began wiggling happily in her arms. "There, there, baby. Mama's fine. I heard about the fire on my drive in from work and feared you could be inside the apartment with a raging fire." She looked up at Green-eyes. "I was so afraid, Lulu."

"It's okay, Ms. Gilmore. I—" She shot him a glance from beneath shuttered eyelashes. Very long, cinnamon lashes. "I was walking him. He heard the sirens and we were close enough to the apartments to see the fire was here and he just took off. Drug me down the street as he tried to get to the apartments. I think he must have been coming to save you or something. He's chased squirrels before but never this. It's a wonder I held on." She grimaced. "Brad—I mean, Fire Chief Sinclair got in the way and I lost hold of him."

"Oh, you sweet dog, coming to rescue me. Thank you, Lulu. I'm forever grateful to you. Now, come on,

Sebastian, let's go get out of the firemen's way so they can do their job."

Got in her way?

Dex looked at Brad and hefted a muscled shoulder. "I'll go check on the men's progress, Chief. Maybe you need to stay out of the way," he muttered and grinned.

"Thanks," Brad ground out, perplexed by the woman's reaction to him. He recognized her, having seen her walking dogs but she always seemed to be heading in a different direction than him. There were a few times he'd spotted her and thought she'd avoided him on purpose. But, other than her red hair, she really wasn't his type and he'd not had any desire to actively pursue anyone since Katie dropped him. He'd dated a lot but he'd never been the pursuer. So, there had been no desire on his part to actually wonder what the dog walker's problem with him was. Now, however, she stared at him as if he'd just tackled her and thrown her to the ground and trampled her. And he needed to understand why she had this reaction. "Did you say you live here?"

"Yes. I-I do live here. Is it bad?" She stepped

away from him, still looking as if she were half afraid of him.

"We got here in time and were able to confine it to the one apartment. Number Four A."

Her eyes flew wide. *"Four A*—that's my apartment. H-how bad? What caused it? Oh no, it wasn't something I did, was it?"

"No, nothing you did. Looks like faulty wiring. These are old apartments."

She glanced around him and her mouth dropped open as she saw the blackened hole that had been her apartment. Windows were broken out and soot encased the brick.

"I'm sorry. Looks like it will be a total loss for you."

Her face fell. "Oh, I see." Instead of bursting into tears like most people did, she closed her mouth, seemed to suck in a deep breath and accept it. As if she was used to accepting bad information on a regular basis. She rubbed her forehead with two fingers. "Okay, I better let you get back to what you were doing. You don't need me getting in your way anymore than I already have. Hopefully no one else has much damage." Then, without waiting, she spun and hurried away.

He watched her disappear into the crowd. Her reaction baffled him. She was definitely different.

"Chief, we need you over here," one of his men called and he went back to work. He needed to get this figured out and then talk to the apartment owner. They were lucky this hadn't been worse but he needed an inspection to make sure the rest of the wiring was up to code or else they might not be so lucky next time. As it was, the dog walker was going to be out an apartment until hers was cleaned up. And she'd be very lucky if she salvaged anything. He hoped the complex had an extra apartment open.

Not his business. His business was putting out the fire, figuring out what started it, and making sure the place was safe going forward.

Still, as he headed back toward the burned-out apartment, his thoughts were with the baffling dog walker.

More Books by Debra Clopton

About the Author

Bestselling author Debra Clopton has sold over 2.5 million books. Her book OPERATION: MARRIED BY CHRISTMAS has been optioned for an ABC Family Movie. Debra is known for her contemporary, western romances, Texas cowboys and feisty heroines. Sweet romance and humor are always intertwined to make readers smile. A sixth generation Texan she lives with her husband on a ranch deep in the heart of Texas. She loves being contacted by readers.

Visit Debra's website at www.debraclopton.com

Sign up for Debra's newsletter at
www.debraclopton.com/contest/

Check out her Facebook at
www.facebook.com/debra.clopton.5

Follow her on Twitter at @debraclopton

Contact her at debraclopton@ymail.com

If you enjoyed reading *Longing for Forever* I would appreciate it if you would help others enjoy this book, too.

Recommend it. Please help other readers find this book by recommending it to friends, reader's groups and discussion boards.

Review it. Please tell other readers why you liked this book by reviewing it on the retail site you purchased it from or Goodreads. If you do write a review, please send an email to debraclopton@ymail.com so I can thank you with a personal email. Or visit me at: www.debraclopton.com.